Ani

Joseph Warren Morris

New Branch Publishing
7454 Huntwick Trail
Nashville, TN 3722
Email: newbranchpublishing@gmail.com
Phone: 615-646-0755

Ani

First published by New Branch Publishing

ISBN 978-0-9988528-8-1

Book design by Jera Publishing

Printed by Lightning Source

Printed in the United States of America
Nashville, Tennessee

Preface

It was a time when the great wars besieged Armenia and Rolande Roscilli had gone there from across the Adriatic to fight in these upheavals as a mercenary soldier. Ani, a strikingly beautiful baby, was born to Rolande and Penelope Roscilli, two lovers, with her mother soon dying in Rolande's arms of infectious influenza. Rolande, bewildered and distraught, gathered his wits and with the aid of his soldier comrades boarded a ship with his baby girl snuggled in a cradle bound for his native Padua, a city in the northern quadrant of Italy.

Welcomed by the people as a heroic countryman for his service in battle he more so was lavishly praised for his care and diligence of a precious baby while crossing a wide, if not dangerous sea. At once, the good people gazed upon this precious baby with inquisitiveness and then with adoration, intimating to one another that strangely there was an aura of mystery about her, something magnetic, something unexplainable. And then there arose a buzz without let up among them. "Did she come, or was she sent, to lift from our presence the scourge just past which is by comparison as terrible as a plague?" The land had suffered for two agonizing years through a stifling drought, the fields crusted over and the lakes and streams without water.

Years passed. Ani had grown into a beauty. In time, decades later, perhaps a century or two, a visitor, a young soldier of the great World War I, traveled to the Roscilli mansion as a guest, discovering an alluring portrait, a life size portrait, that hung conspicuously in a secluded room of great expanse and had hung there he would learn for a time of some immensity. Suddenly an obsession with this enchanting girl, herself youthful, swept upon him. Helpless to escape its grip, night after night he returned to observe and be with her, ceaselessly pondering her heritage and why she now stayed fixed in that artistic frame appended to the wall of a towering solitary room. And for how long, it ran through him, had she resided there? But at last, the mystery was unraveled. "Ah! I see it now. She is Rolande's and Penelope's daughter. She is Ani. She surely is Ani."

Chapter 1

IT WAS 1918. I had been drafted. There was a war nearing four years of length, approaching its end, a war that historians, journalists, and statesmen alike called World War I, which largely encompassed the United States, Great Britain, France and Italy on the one hand and Germany, Austria/Hungary and Turkey on the other. It was a savage war, millions of soldiers died on both sides of the fighting, many blown to bits by cannon fire, or felled by rapid delivery weaponry, or perhaps even more horribly died from suffocation which resulted from the use of chemically produced gas by either adversary. Lady luck had smiled my way, for I entered the scene of battle as a medic only two months in advance of the declaration of an armistice and was never ordered to front line duty.

I would not return immediately with the bulk of troops back to America, assigned at this interim to a military hospital in central

France for assisting in the care and convalescence of soldiers too badly injured for physical removal from the bed in which they lay. With little expiration of time, a short while after the armistice, I along with a trickle of others from the medical staff were granted furlough for a brevity —two weeks I think it was—for visiting some of the more culturally recognized adornments of Europe, or otherwise to choose our own sites of attraction. I had met a young medic from Italy, a Giovanni Roscilli, of virtually my age who had served with me as a fellow staffer since my arrival, who asked me to accompany him to the whereabouts of his birth to meet his family who now worried, he said, of his well being.

"And where is it they live?"

"Near Padua, Padua, Italy, an exceedingly old city situated in the northern sector of the Peninsula. I must tell you though, my friend, that I speak of Padua as my home somewhat erringly. I should say more pertinently that my actual home is nestled in a farming community in the vicinity of Padua. One might say on the outskirts. I am of a family of farmers. We grow wheat, and corn, and grapes. The city itself is situated on the banks of the river Bacchiglione."

We caught the train to our destination, to Padua, which I detected beforehand by use of a road map that it lay southwest of my base in France not less than a half day's ride, not an unusual time of travel considering that the train moved at a drudgingly slow rate of speed and made constant stops while enroute. When we arrived, my notice fell instantly on what my friend had said to me pursuant to the city's age, indeed old. In many ways it still reflected its past, a community of changing fortunes, for example its economic and territorial expansion and magnificent works of art and science—but more than anything else the evidence suggested that it was once a community of castle towns. We stayed but few hours then traveled a short distance to his family's home, where the father and mother kissed their son lavishly while teardrops wafted softly down their faces and extended a gladdened welcome to me together with a delight at meeting face to face their son's good friend. "These are educated people," I internalized to myself," born of high culture which I determined beforehand through my affiliation with their son." He hadn't so far revealed the extent of his family's wealth and the high place they occupied in local society but that would soon start to evince itself in my grasp of understanding."

The home towered three stories in height, was comprised of what seemed an endless number of rooms, and exhibited a style of architecture that sprang from another age, two centuries coming to me as a reasonable estimation. The exterior stone, Gothic, was of a darkened hue, a plethora of small windows appearing out at you through the heavy thick walls, excepting one, a very large one, so expansive that a person standing on the interior could sweepingly see for miles across the landscape of meadows and fields of agriculture. Both the exterior and interior doors were constructed of hardened oak, well finished and shiny, the work of a master artisan.

"Before we get settled in," said my friend, "I shall show you through the interior, then we'll dine afterwards and then tonight trade stories. Tomorrow we'll saddle the horses and trek across the fields, or venture into old Padua. But as I have just said we shall explore the interior, which is now."

"By all means. Lead me as you wish."

I determined upon first glimpsing the inside that my eyes were witnessing the remnants of a past grandeur, where noblemen of a different age sat at the gargantuan oaken table and toasted and drank and exacted strategies of awesome war. We were at this moment in the breakfast room, still the breakfast room after centuries of use at the very least, protected and perpetuated for future familial generations. We went along, through rooms of capacious size, which were many, endless I thought. We did not hurry, merely browsing and musing, staying long lengths in one place so that I might study and admire an attraction that beheld me. Some few ottomans and golden candelabra caught my alert and busy eyes as we approached the east side and after we had gone further, I began to take notice that all doors were left open, save one, which stayed permanently closed, I conjectured, but at the time there was no reason why such an oddity, if there was one, merited consideration. Ah! There on the lofty walls, gigantic in height, hung draperies of the richest tapestry from summit to foot in an attitude of vast folds. I scanned the vaulting, immense, measuring to my way of guessing to a height of thirty or more feet from floor level, constructed and engineered of such design that a mere whisper sounded as an echo. At this juncture we had seen much and truthfully, after we had toured just under two hours I yet anticipated a continuance, an expectation that my friend would have gladly honored but for dinner which the butler had momentarily announced. So, my friend suggested that we terminate the tour until later, not specifying when we might resume.

The home was to me so immensely large for a family of two that I fell into wondering why this was so. But my friend, perhaps reading my puzzlement, explained that two others of the family were away, his brother, a slight older than himself, and a sister two years younger.

We sat for dinner. It was served by the butler assisted by a middle aged woman who wore a glossy white apron, but said nothing. She only smiled and did as the butler gestured. The father sat at the end of the table, the mother to his right and my friend to his left. I sat by my friend. My hosts, the parents that is, talked but speciously of the history of this great family, more so of our present experiences in the army. He too spoke gratefulness that both of us were trained medics and thereby were confined to medical duties as opposed to the hard and dangerous life of a foot soldier. The mother issued similar remarks. As part of the conversation the father alluded to the harvesting of the crops now and then while the mother proudly gave narrations of the rich and exotic paintings, mostly of people in pose, hanging plentifully throughout the hallways and other conspicuous places. Brought up also was the subject of his son whom he proudly said had studied under a renowned doctor in Vienna, Austria and that the field of medicine would reward us well throughout our lives if we stuck with it. And this was largely the topics of discussion at dinner for the duration of our stay. I generally listened, asking a few questions from to time, but cautiously and politely done.

After dinner, we rose and bade goodnight to the parents and went to our rooms on the second floor, my room next to my friend's, both rooms, it did not escape me, bearing a coat of arms immediately above the doorway Which betold that his family in addition to its remarkable success in the enterprise of agriculture had been also a family of soldiers. It was here in this wondrous edifice that we stayed a full week and where my friend began and finished a story that I have retained until this day, being by now substantially of old age. It occurred on occasions that he chose to return to a fragment of narrative previously told, each time repeating the lines over and over with hardly a syllable of change from one telling to the next.

"My friend," he would commence, "my family tree dates back not over decades but centuries, at least a few, and this home has been owned and occupied in that span by the same family strain. The story that I am about to pass to you I have consumed by reading scores of documentations and listening to tales told by this or that kindred as my years have progressed and derives from and because of a young soldier of an earlier family of relatives who went to battle in some foreign domain across the waters. Being something of a renegade, I judge, he had volunteered for pay as a mercenary fighter"

"Bought."

"Precisely."

"No one seems certain of the exactness of the where or when of his embattlement, except to suggest in a manner of conjecture that it took place in the lower quadrant of the Adriatic Sea or in some territory across the Mediterranean, perhaps in Armenia, Syria, Lebanon, Cyprus, Turkey, such sovereignties forming the region which is now spoken of as the Levant in the pages of the books of geography. It seems that he fought in each of these domains at some time or the other, although the documentations in the family storages speak convincingly that he foremostly did so in Armenia. As I said, no one knows exactly of the where or when of his circumstance. They only know what legend has said that has crept forward over the expanse of time.

"Do you not know his name?"

"Forgive my omission. I should have said that it was Rolande. It says so in the old family Bible."

He seemed to begin a silent furtherance of that which some family member had mentioned of Rolande. Suddenly he continued.

"It was established by letters and by other similar communicants—a notation even in the family Bible here and there—that prior to his going off to war he seriously entertained notions of wedding a Louisa Adriane, a splendid girl of our community whom he professed to love dearly; and there was reason to believe that those were his deeply ingrained sentiments. Nevertheless, after exchanging the pros and cons of the wedding under the existing conditions they agreed jointly and affably to postpone the wedding until he returned from the field of battle. So, he bade her goodbye and sailed away and entered the war abroad.

Chapter 2

SOLDIERS AFTER A period of physical combat must of necessity rest from such encounters and just as you and I are now enjoying an escape from military activity so too his commander relieved him and a limitation of his fellow soldiers from duty from time to time. This was likely for but a few days for each furlough, but whichever it was they seemed to have ventured aimlessly in their respite of leisure into the mountainous villages not of great length from the perimeter of fighting, there intermingling with the native locals. He often thought of Louisa during these jaunts of idleness but he suffered from loneliness, particularly if he let his mind wander in retrospect to the rapture of her kisses. As a consequence, he one day struck up an acquaintance with an enchanting girl of Armenian vintage. She went by the name of Penelope. She too was lonely and sought comfort from this young affable soldier and he from her, as one might deem natural. His visits to the mountains increased from a few to many, their hearts beginning to warm for one another more so with each visit and thus a baby girl was born unto them, to whom they gave the name Ani, meaning very beautiful in the Armenian vernacular. Even as a baby she was a beauty of rarity. The parents were greatly happy when first looking upon her. One can imagine that in his frenzy of elation Rolande easily repressed his attachment to Louisa. All throughout the village the good folks rejoiced with the young parents and could only see their future filled with blessings; yet fate too often intervenes with an unfettered plan for charting an unexpected course. Crushing to his heart the young mother died in his arms of infectious influenza breaking out and killing her only three weeks after the birthing of Ani.

Bewildered and distraught Rolande nevertheless gathered his wits, quickly realizing the predicament in which he found himself and with little waste thought of Penelope's family, wishing they were still alive. 'I could turn to them. They would help me. And possibly for a short while take custody of the infant.' There was no family, none, all killed in the ravages of war and had died some months before his meeting Penelope, whereupon their death she now, young as she was, faced the harsh extremity of fending for herself."

"Ah! Pitiable."

"You have spoken for us both. But let us go on. There was no one to take care of the baby, he had concluded, except himself, and with steely resolve avowed never to give her up to another's custody. Though short of seasoning and maturity Rolande had more than subtly discovered by now that Ani had become to him a part of his very soul, precious beyond description. Yet he had erred in his judgment of others, for his soldier comrades stepped forward with unbending commitment to help see him through his ordeal, and soon they, in conjunction with the kind sisters of a monastery nearby, contrived an arrangement for him and his daughter to board a sea going vessel whose chartings would take them across the broad Mediterranean and then the Adriatic, and from there to the coastal port of northern Italy near Padua. But I must add here that if it were not the case that Rolande's commanding general had not been sympathetic to the plight of both Ani and her young father, thereby giving his unrelenting support to the scheme of things, the mission might well have failed. As it happened, the general delighted at seeing his troops, ruffians by their very nature and life's accords, lovingly take the infant to their hearts and with playful mirth feeding and bathing and medicating and holding and pampering her with assiduous care. Much to everyone's amazement, particularly to his troops, the general led everyone in prayer, therein making mention that despite the death of the beloved Penelope the rest of all else surely was divinely inspired."

I spoke thusly. "Surely it was tiresome and lengthy of days to cross the two great seas before they reached the shores of Rolande's native Italy. How was it that he cared for the baby infant during this stretch of his sojourn?"

"Ha. The commanding general wielded great power, holding jurisdiction over the navies as well as the land forces, including the ship's captain and members of the crew. His instructions, commands in actuality, came forth that the ship's crew was to duplicate the steps taken by the land soldiers in caring for the infant and such orders were followed to the letter. But let me go on lest I lose where I am in my story. And already I have left something of vital importance unsaid."

"Yes, yes. Please continue."

"When the ship was setting sail Rolande raised his face skyward and commended himself to the Good Lord in Heaven to see after and give to him assistance in every way necessary for now he must face the wide waters of both seas with a helpless babe—he shuddered I will suppose—and must eventually kneel humbly before Louisa with an explanation of the experiences he had undergone, which she upon hearing him out would shockingly condemn. While as expected Louisa as well as the good people of the community reacted with obstinacy but reached in their hearts and forgave, though in some large measure because by now they were overcome by this angelic gift from far away overseas and considering as they did that Rolande, a native son, had placed his life in harms way on behalf of his country declared him a hero. But was heralded more generously because here he was, still a mere youth, who had unbelievingly nurtured and in every necessary manner cared for an infant over a long and perilous journey. Not in the least can I leave out Louisia who with purity and kindness of heart took Rolande back into fold, in turn giving her hand to him in marriage and adopting the baby Ani as her very own."

I breathed a sigh. "What an unexpected ending."

"You are speaking of Louisa's forgiveness of Rolande and in the end joining him in marriage."

"Well, that in and of itself warrants a particular incisiveness. Yet that is not what I have reference to."

"Then what? What do you have reference to?"

"It's about something you said just a moment ago. You made mention that the good people turned their adoration to Ani, the precious little babe, intimating to one another that strangely she seemed to possess an unexplainable power, magnetic and mysterious—not because of the rarity of her beauty but, but, because, because—!"

"Let me finish for you. It's been said that when she came to them the people when first gazing upon her were instantly overwhelmed with awe, by the aura about her, something messianic, allow me to say, for suddenly out of nowhere she had popped up —most odd, most unexplainable their minds must have been messaging—and that they believed or wanted to believe that she had come, or was sent, to lift from their presence a plight almost as terrible as a plague.

"My gracious." I crossed myself. "You stretch my imagination."

"Perhaps you should not go to that extreme and will not I surmise after you have heard me out."

"Heard you out?"

"Yes. You see, something had descended upon them quite terrible, as I have said just now."

"Something tantamount to a plague. And what was that exactly?"

"It was the land. It had to do with the land, which was then stricken for two years in succession with a stifling drought, no rain, the fields crusted over and plants withered to a crisp and food for the tables drastically reduced. Dust everywhere spread. Prayers were delivered for relief, people jointly gathering in vigils beseeching the Heavens to summon the appearance of dark clouds to form and drench their fields and thereby yield up widespread helpfulness. Very soon, within two days after Rolande and Ani's arrival, the clouds meshed and foamed and burst open, flooding the fields and filling the streams and lakes and at last ended the suffering of a people long under anxiety and stress, whose hope had dangerously neared the end of its course. 'The baby. Our precious gift,' they whispered to one another. 'Is it possible that she is a blessing from Heaven come to pull us back from the precipice of despair and ruin.'"

"Astounding!" I felt a temptation to utter that this fantastic dissimulation coming from his lips equated with stories of gypsy tales that I had at some time or another read of, or seen acted out on stage. No, I did not do that, choosing instead a different option. "I find my friend that it is not easy for me to respond, except I do wonder if they in fact truly believed in what they were saying, or in fact were they simply caught up in a grip of fantasy?"

"You question. But I am in the likeness of yourself. It does not seem natural that they would believe, or could believe, yet on the other hand consider this: when one is mired in almost a pitiable circumstance, with no way of escape and is pressed to the brink of extinction, he may well grasp at the thinnest straw within reach."

"So, he might." I paused for a brevity, examining my thoughts, still aghast at the fantasticness of the story that had come to me, then went on. "It falls upon me presumptuously that the fields once again flourished and provided sustenance as before, and this surely evoked stupendous rejoicing among the people. In my mind's eye I can see them now kneeling and rendering thanks to the Lord for lifting their burden and not withstanding always whispering the name of Ani in their utterances."

"You have phrased it well, or in any event much in the likeness of how I too see it."

At this intermission, though enthralled at the miracle that my friend had described, my thoughts and imaginings had begun to fall most singularly and subtly on Ani of which I had started to draw more and more into awareness, if but vaguely, and as the story further unfolded her image and persona pressed upon me with increasing intrigue, even though I only knew and saw her through the words seeping into my ears. I then asked my friend what happened to her, meaning of course as she became older.

"She grew up, as you have inferred in your question. But you deserve better than such a curt answer. Help me understand therefore what you are especially seeking."

"Can you speak with relative certainty of her life's progression, most poignantly of her early life and its attendant aspects, which you have so far absented? I presume that you know much more of her than you have heretofore laid bare."

He did not pause.

"I call your attention to what has seemed glaringly obvious through documentations over time, old faded letters, yellowing pages from the family Bibles, written notes meticulously inscribed, speaking's of the mouth and so on, that she evolved into greater beauty with each passing day. I could virtually recite from some if not most of these documentations. But it is here however that

I recuse myself in favor of a manuscript of a sort prepared and detailed by a lady long extinct whose name was Mazurka Bravino, a person of gifted penmanship, who lived in Ani's time, and was so attracted by the beauty of this darling girl that she described it in words and said much of her otherwise. I have read this manuscript repeatedly, many times, which is now virtually unusable. I strained my eyes yet failed to interpret a substantial quantity of her adjectives and narrations, the adjectives most particularly. Luckily, someone, name unknown to me, possessed the wisdom and foresight to copy the original and it is this version in part which I now read to you. Said Madame Bravino—."

Chapter 3

AS SHE GREW older, in the proximity of ten years of age or thereabouts, Ani became increasingly curious of her past. "Who was my mother? From whence did she come?" and to whom could she depend for an answer unless it were her beloved father to whom she clung to as does moss to a stone, with Rolande responding to the best that his memory allowed. He recalled that Penelope conveyed to him in bits and pieces that the son of an Italian ambassador to Spain had met her mother while on a climbing venture in the Pyrenees in the southern region of France, that they became lovers, Penelope got born and the young father returned to Italy, never heard from again. Said Rolande, "I learned very little about Penelope's mother. She died so young, very quickly after Penelope was born."

"Ah! Did her mother have relatives, someone to help her?"

"I supposed she had relatives—several I venture—in any event cousins, uncles, sisters, but kindred that I never knew or knew of."

"This you have shared with me my father and I am grateful. Yet I thirst for more."

"More?"

"Yes. Tell me of other things about you and my mother, what you did together, of what your first meeting with her was like?"

"Let me think. Where shall I begin? Yes, I know where. Soon after my meeting her, in fact after the very first one, she came to the military post, knowing somehow that she could get food without obligation. Perhaps I had told her she could. I'm sure I did, for I knew that it was in my grasp to see to it that no one imposed a denial of her need. A friend could work wonders with those in charge of food stuffs, the quartermaster and cooks, especially the cooks, who boasted openly that they were the best at their trade in any quadrant, and they were, their recipes unmatchable throughout the whole of the sovereignty I am willing to wager. Taking advantage of such vanity we met with no trouble at enticing those good fellows to pack pounds of chicken and mutton and vegetables of the multiple sorts into a tote basket which we carried into the mountains for Penelope and friends."

"Ah! I wish I had been there with you."

'At this Rolande laughed and drew her preciously to him.'

"You are a wonder; you are an angel." And then. "You have asked what our life was like together. First, there is a restriction. I cannot allow Louisa to hear certain things in this connection but you are my darling daughter and are entitled to know everything.

So, I will begin. I often recall the nights that I spent with her in the mountains. One night the moon shone with a brilliance, looking as if it were a piece of gold as it climbed over the eastern rim and the air exuded a more than usual coldness. Snow had fallen, literally wrapping itself around the base of the towering pines that grew as mushrooms across the landscape. We kept the fire going throughout the night, never sleeping, perking coffee in a metal pot of antiquated character and eating pepper spiced beans cooked in a blackish steel kettle that hung by way of two wires fastened to a wooden pole. I would look at her for hours in the moonlight. She drew me as compellingly as a magnet draws a piece of metal. When the flames began to die their shadows rose and fell, dancing across her lovely face. There was something about her eyes, so beautiful, magical, mysterious.

Then there is another instance suddenly coming to me that you may fain well appreciate hearing and assuming that you will I shall take the liberty to go into it, but I will only allude to it briefly. We had camped out. I left her momentarily, going a short few steps over to toss chunks of wood and limbs on the fire, staying but a pittance, as I have inferred, when she playfully called out, Rolande I shiver in this cold, come back and share with me the blankets, and I would hurry back to her."

"Playmates. You were like children."

"Yes. Children. That's who we were."

'Ani said nothing for the longest, her mouth a little opened and face filled with fascination and wonder. I think for a moment she had gone back in time through the magic of fantasy. Was it her mother she thought of; was it her mother that she had just met?'

"There is more that over time I will relay to you, but for now I have told enough, excepting an allusion to my courtship with your mother which led to your birth. And, and, I—."

"My birth. And she died very soon afterward."

"Three weeks."

"What did you do about me my father? You were a mere soldier, a young boy, surely frightened quite awfully, and with no clear mapping in your head as to how you might attend to the infant child in your possession."

"That is so, very so. But there was one thing I knew my sweet and wonderful child above all other things. As surely as the sun rises each morning in the east, I could have never left you behind in far away Armenia any more than I could have taken leave of my very soul.'"

"And that is all of Madame Mazurka Bravino for now. Let us if you will remove ourselves for a few moments to another course of the story of Ani."

"I will listen with rapt attention. Please go on."

"The women of the community, as well as the men folks, so much loved to hear these stories. Now which do you suppose they loved the most?"

"Of those I have heard thus far?"

"Exactly."

"I haven't the faintest." I wavered my head and gave forth a chuckle, thinking silently that he had instituted a game of sort at this juncture so as to whet my appetite for listening. Then I repeated. "I haven't the faintest."

"Let me take you back. Recall if you will that somewhere in the foregoing, I have pointed out that as Ani increased in years she evolved or was evolving into yet a greater beauty, possibly estimating that at this stage she had attained to an age of twenty years. I have read as much in this or that documentation and if my measure is decently reliable the people spoke more of her in this period than in any other."

"Spoke of her beauty I take it you mean to say."

"I meant that."

"How beautiful was she? My curiosity has peaked to its loftiest pinnacle."

"I know what was written, a piece on a tablet sheet and signed Anonymous, which you surmise was Madame Bravino. But I do not think so. If it had been her work Madame Bravino would have signed in declaration of ownership. Someone else I strongly deduce had to write it, a distant cousin of hers I suspect who'd fallen madly in love with her, but never admitting that passions of that intensity and nature ran through him. I believe that at this interval he was enrolled in one of the universities of Paris."

"Do you have possession of this document?"

"I so have it before me, anticipating this moment last evening, thereupon retrieving it from the family storages. And I now will read portions of it to you."

"'Her stature is of the average height, a compellingly graceful height. In beauty of face, I do not believe there is an equal, and that was so beginning when she was but an infant. Her features are not even faintly of the regular mold, this being, among other attractants, that there is something of a quiet strangeness in her persona, the same endowment showing in her mother Penelope. One is drawn instantly to her raven black fleeces, luxuriant and naturally curling, as they dangle about her shoulders.

And ah! Here I mention it once more. There is that immaculate face, smooth and without flaw, and then her sweet mouth, indeed the triumph of all things Heavenly. Do I dare omit other features? I do not. The hue of her eyes is of the most brilliant of black, her skin luminously white, and soft and lovely, and during the summer months she leaves the upper portions of her arms unclothed and exposed. Such is the erectness of her carriage that one wonders if she is taught by a tutor. I have looked at the forehead, perfect in its design, and then of all things at the delicate outlines of her nose, thereby retreating into flight to recall a poet declaring that nowhere but in the graceful medallions of the Hebrews had he beheld a similar perfection.'"

"How brilliantly put," I said, "a poetic masterpiece. But allow me if you will dear friend. You mentioned that he in effect had fallen passionately in love with Ani and that this had driven him to the extremity of madness. Did you literally mean that was so?"

"Family legend says as much. It appears in the documentations."

"Thank you." And then he continued.

Chapter 4

"I HAVE ANOTHER ACCOUNTING of Madame Bravino's notations that I have not heretofore mentioned," my friend informed, "alluding's that aren't meant to have a great deal to do with Ani's looks of beauty but largely with a trip across the family's vast land holdings that she experienced with Ani, and I gladly share them with you. The readings may pose difficulty to you in places due to the fading of print and paper but by and large I think you'll make everything out suitably well."

"Thank you." I said again and began to read Madame Bravino's second narration.

'It was my joy and good fortune to receive approval to accompany Ani across the vast acreage of farmlands, a trip on which we departed early, shortly after sunrise, realizing that a considerable while was in the making in order to transcend the entire expanse.

We would not cover it all. But would get in as much sight seeing as daylight permitted. I more than welcomed the opportunity to go along, in fact felt honored. I had heard that she, as well as the family, permitted but few outside the immediate household to ride with her no matter where she went. I was lucky. She had learned to like me. I knew that. She selected the sorrel for herself, a strong spirited animal that few others could handle, sometimes rearing up and refusing to go as the rider directed—but he behaved calmly and obediently under her command. They got along well, her understanding him and him understanding her. The mount chosen for me was endowed of a tame and gentle disposition and on him I felt assuredly secure.

She looked breathtaking in her riding attire, likened to a breath of spring, so beautiful in the fullness of the sun, a vested blouse of black and white fitted over her torso, with ruffles appropriately spaced, a small hat or beret perched coquettishly on her head and coal black strands falling strikingly about her shoulders. Apparent also were her riding pants, coal black in the manner of her strands, and so too were her riding boots, the extreme upper portions reaching to her knees. Beginning to feel the coldness of the morning she suddenly unbundled a heavily lined woolen jacket and put it on. I hated to see her cover up her riding attire. She was so gorgeous in it. Already I wore a fur coat that dropped to my knees.

We set out, the sun beginning to push slowly higher into the eastern sky, happy and joyful at the clear gorgeous day and I thought to myself how good it was that I was alive and traveling with someone I truly admired and had taken to. Spring had come a month or more before, beautiful, harmoniously, without spring's anticipations, one of those rare springs that brings joy to plants, animals, and people alike. Everything was wonderful, everything was cheerful. I almost broke into an old song that my mother taught me when I was a little girl, and would have were it not for a flock of wild geese flying lowly southward fifty yards from us. "Look, Mrs. Bravino," said Ani excitedly. "See the geese. They're searching for food at some place nearby. They feed upon the various leftover seed in the winter rye fields this time of year." We rode by another field where last year's clover was sewn and harvested and still by another field that had been ploughed and readied for the sewing of spring wheat. The clover sprouting among the stubble was at one and the same time refreshing and inspiring, revived already and steadily greening among the broken stalks of last year's harvest. Ani's mount suddenly decided to go off course and venture into the clover growth, its hoofs making a deep sucking sound as they quickly sank into the muddy ground. Sharply yanking his reins, she spoke a word of displeasure and he seemed to fathom the meaning of her intent, wasting no time at getting back on course. A little later Ani rode her horse across a brook that we had come to, judging that the water from the rain that fell the day before had sufficiently subsided, knowing that it had in that she'd crossed this part of the stream before, perhaps many times, when it was swollen. I followed. There were no other eventualities worth speaking of accepting that we stirred up two ducks and a woodcock from the water, both of us wondering if we were truly seeing a woodcock or some other similar fowl. Shortly we met a woodsman who verified without doubt that we had seen a woodcock. We rode on and had ridden for a while, the sun climbing steadily higher, with me glancing backward in anticipation of seeing the family mansion which appeared no where in sight, disappearing some time ago. We must have traveled by now three to four miles I estimated, a few miles more bringing us to the edge of the heartland and a scattering of village settlements. It was still cold, evinced by the horses blowing a stream of moisture out of their nostrils and so did we. Here and there small wooden houses commenced to appear with narrow crudely made windows peeping outward in which the workers lived who tilled the land and saw after the stock. These were the serfs but no longer serfs from a legal standpoint, the family emancipating them some decades in the past. When they were legally freed, I think I had not been born. As we passed by these houses Ani waived vigorously with arms and hands over her head to the women workers hard at performing their daily chores and upon seeing her dropped everything and made their way over, the younger women on spirited legs, the older ones waddling forward as fast as their older and fat legs allowed but getting there, all of them one by one hugging and taking on over her in a most happy demeanor. Once when we were passing by other houses in another village Ani did not wait for the women to come to her. Sliding from her horse she quickly paced her way over to where they were doing their weekly washing, the women earlier building a fire around and under a giant kettle in which the clothes were now submerged. With unrestrained laughter they gathered her into their arms, whispering the sweetest exclamations, "dear child, you have come to see us. We are so glad." I tried to stifle a smile, and hold my breath simultaneously when Ani unexpectedly clasped a ladle and began to stir the clothes and lift them up and down. "Oh gracious," a middle-aged woman in nearby presence uttered excitedly, "Oh my dearest, please, you might scald your sweet self," meaning in her moment of shock that it was too much that this blessed one should for a second put her hands to common use.

So, we continued with our journey, Ani eager and spirited to go on, elated at the prospect of surveying the ebb and flow of the great acreage of land that sprawled before us. At this stage we began to intercept fewer settlements. It was now well into spring which normally would have ushered in warmer temperature in that part of the morning. The air seemed to have gotten colder. We pulled our top coats tighter to our bodies, Ani explaining that we had ascended to a higher elevation where the wind blew freer and less checked and that this combined with our entering a grove of enormously tall pines, which blotted out the sun, forced a chill to one's skin which we had not recently noticed. But we soon left the pine grove and in a little while the sun had climbed yet ever higher, the air then becoming warmer and we were thankful that nature had smiled down upon us.

The terrain kept rising and falling, sometimes flat and sprawling, at other times billowing and undulating. Ani delighted at seeing the cattle and farm yards as we passed them by, slowing the sorrel to almost a stand still now and then, laughing happily while pointing animatedly at a baby calf scampering energetically among its peers. She said that the cattle pens were moved about intermittently as need be so as to provide manure for the planting of some crop due for planting later in the season, a comment that surprisingly told me she was well schooled in the procedures and processing of soil enrichment. Soon we were passed the settlement and into the open fields again. I kept admiring the finesse with which she handled the sorrel and the way she sat in her saddle, so statuesque, swaying rhythmically to the amble of her proud and haughty steed. By now the pattern of the landscape had changed significantly. She sighed at the patches of snow still clinging to the top soil even though at this interim of spring none of it should have so stubbornly stuck around. We again began to approach and ride through another grove of tall trees, spruce and aspen swaying in the breeze, much taller than any trees we had yet seen. I marveled at the beauty of the aspen, with bark of shiny white from bottom to top dotting the hills and ridges off in the distance. After a while we emerged from the woods onto the edge of a field of rankish young wheat, the winter variety, which spread before us in the likeness of a smooth velvety carpet, interrupted here and there by low shady places where the remains of snow yet stubbornly held on. The workers would come in early summer with scythes in hand to mow the wheat and haul it to market for sale. They were a happy lot, always singing old folk songs that dated back for hundreds of years. It was obvious that the landscape had become appreciably hillier, a landmark that Ani decided to use for our making a turnaround for home, saying in the same breath however that we should first have lunch and then went and removed a leather satchel strapped to her horse's saddle. She had packed it with food and drink. The drink I have forgotten, but not the food, an assortment of ham and biscuits, a cut of cheese, a bit of raw fruit, and a slice of cake. All this, in its digestive process, left her with the need for a nap and thereupon she dropped to her knees in preparation of prayer.

Then she crossed herself and uttered reverence to her Lord, lying down at once under a bush and putting together a mesh of soft green grass for her pillow. Soon she fell off to sleep. As she slept, she seemed so at rest as I looked down upon her, so much at peace with the world, her breast lifting and descending with silent ease, her face that of an angel. And then it struck me. Don't they say that she is not only beautiful, that she is spiritually beautiful? And that is the greatest beauty of all. I had always believed that. But now I believed it even more as I studied her sleeping face, at which I kept on looking for a long while. She had prayed just before lying down. I didn't. I met her as I recall in Saint Anthony's Basilica of Padua where she attended either the morning or evening Mass. That was the first I ever saw her, a young beautiful girl and in a strange way so different from others I thought to myself, different in a way that I now cannot justifiably describe as she knelt at the alter in prayer, her face turned upward toward the icon Mary, her eyes closed, her hands cupped together. She was dressed in old Italian white lace. If the Lord ever blesses anyone, it ran through me, he surely smiles down and blesses her.

She had fallen to sleep at once after lying down and awakened only when the sun had passed on the other side of the bush and stolen lightly across her face, instantly waking her. Yawning, she sat up, smiled over at me and gave a little sigh, uttering apologetically that she had slept too long and that now we must without delay start our way back, for sundown would fall upon us sooner than we might think and then we remounted.

Ani had decided to alter the routing back home, choosing to traverse northward toward a stream, I know not the name, which flowed from the foothills of the mountain range which lay eastward into a larger stream thrice fold the size of its smaller sibling, then passing near the family mansion and eventually emptying into the Adriatic. This larger stream we in time would intercept, the waters rolling and tumbling, the resultant effect of the heavy rains that fell the night before in the higher elevations. Ani remarked that they appeared quite angry.

'Savage,' I quipped.

"Yes savage," she chirped, smiling in agreement.

It amused her when I enlarged upon what she had said.

She spoke that we must cross this stream at some point further in the continuance of our journey at a shoals of which she was knowledgeable—but that this was not the place, obviously. The waters were too turbulent. And thus we rode on. The shoreline did not pose difficulty of any consequence, no thickets or other gnarlments obstructing our pathway. But there were trees, tall and majestic trees, pine and oak and aspen and a witch helm here and there, laden with growth so profoundly abundant that we could hardly see the dappling of the sun rippling through. I feared that I might incur a crick in my neck. I had stood looking upward for some time without pause at this fantastic presence of nature. Ani chose the description for me. "The work of Heaven!"

'Ah yes! What else?'

She then mentioned that the sun had now dropped markedly in comparison to its position when we set out homeward. I nodded agreement.

Within an hour or thereabouts she drew her mount to a halt and called out that we had descended upon the shoals, the stream here spreading out in the shape of a fan, the width much greater, and therefore the waters calmer and of much less depth. Even before reaching this point, I had begun to sense that the shoals were of short distance ahead because the roar of the water had subsided to a level only vaguely audible to my hearing. It was here that we took pause, letting the horses rest and drink, and then thereafter cross to the other side. She explained with a detectable glimmer of joy that after finishing with the crossing we would then pursue a course westward across the flatlands and then from there come to the end of our destination. I mounted first and guided my horse into the swirl, assuming without looking back that Ani closely trailed, an assumption that failed to materialize. When she had gotten into her saddle and issued the simple command for her horse to proceed forward, she suddenly was met with complete surprise. The horse snorted and reared up, refusing to take one step. 'What on earth,' it must have raced through her. 'What can this mean?' But here she would show her metal, her true character and with great patience commenced to talk to the animal in the gentlest of tone, never once threatening or scolding. I looked upon the scene with exasperation. What could I do to help I wondered? 'Nothing,' I advised myself and sat helplessly in my saddle observing. "What has gotten into him?" But speculated that it was something he saw in the waters, or heard, swiftly passing over the rocks. The animal was unnerved, moved by something unexplainable, certainly to me, and I could tell by looking into her face that to her the cause also remained a mystery. But she stayed calm, in not an iota ruffled. After another try, or perhaps another, but without success she slid slowly from her saddle, took firmly hold of the reins, dead set on winning the battle between beauty and beast which was now at play. I chuckled. Leading him on or attempting to I should say she now spoke as if speaking to a child but of a few years of age, soothing, pleading, encouraging, all this in the softest of tones, "Come on, come on," simultaneously patting and caressing his forehead while smoothing her hand up and down his powerful neck. I looked again into her face, focused, steady, calm, controlling, and all the while speaking reassuringly. I think he suddenly felt ashamed. Were he able to talk human talk I'm convinced that he would have admitted as much. I almost clapped when seeing her move away without him he efforted a tiny step forward then griped convulsively and from there with forelegs stepping quickly up and down, as would a majorette leading a marching band, partly lunged and partly high stepped through the waters to the opposite shore. I don't recall Ani saying one word, just climbing into her saddle and signaling by way of moving lightly the reins that all was well again and that we must go on.

From there we retraced ourselves, moving away from the stream that lay cradled in a valley by rounded hills in the distance, emerging in a while onto the sprawling flatlands through which we had traveled during the morning hours. In shorter time than I realized the sun had dropped closer to the impending horizon. Ani tapped the shoulders of her mount with her riding strap hurrying him into a trot. Without her telling me I knew then that internally she raced against nightfall, hoping to reach home by sunset. I surmised that nightfall or a mite after was the more probable goal. She was a calm one under any circumstance, I could vouch for that, never exhibiting a sign of uneasiness in the time entire that I had known her, only the reverse qualities, an unalterable composure and good judgment, and I don't think it bothered her an iota's worth that we could find ourselves caught in the darkness. She knew her way as well as she knew the back of her hand. While I had declined to make mention of it at first, I had begun to see figures of men on the edge of the woods now and then or else thought I had, appearing to dart back among the trees when they determined that I had caught them in my sight. On relaying this to Ani I met the unaffected reply that these were men of a close by settlement, who on instructions from her family were to vigilantly see that she at no time ever got lost, or endangered by wild animals, or worse still approached by unsavory people.

We were now out into the open, moving away from the tree line and into the farming sector. Touching him with her riding strap Ani asked her mount to pick up the pace, and looked at the sun in its continued descent, and I looked at it too, wishing in some magical way that I could slow its movements.

Eventually we came to another settlement. We'd not seen one since morning. The people recognized her at once, and waving joyfully came running, with her leaning over and grazing their cheeks with her fingers, or bending over almost out of her saddle to kiss this or that old lady. They pled for us to stay longer, to have supper, yet knew that we must journey on and that they shouldn't detain us. It was not long afterwards that we met an old man carting a load of cut firewood, too old my mind told me to undertake such a grueling job. He stopped and so did we. He seemed such a kind old fellow, I thought, and on this I did not err, for no more than a moment after the exchanges between us he asked if perhaps we were off course, and when we replied no, we weren't lost, he nodded and asked further, and I fought hard to suppress my laughter, if we might like to have some food and water to drink. He said the food was dried beef, jerky, that he kept in a leather pouch tied to the siding of his cart. We replied kindly that we were fine with things as they were and bade him goodbye.

'What language does he speak,' I asked Ani. I actually could not tell. He spoke in an accent strange to my hearing. I struggled to understand.

"A mix, something of the language our village folks speak. That's about as much as I can tell you. He was rather difficult to follow, wasn't he? He has his own idiom."

'Ha, ha, ha, ha.' She instantly knew the reason for my laughter and she laughed too. She studied currently at the University of Padua, very much enthralled with the field of arts and languages and had only recently taken up the term with me, mainly because her professor had gone into exhaustive lengths to explain it to his students. He had said to them that an idiom is a saying special to a language and in English for example does not translate to an idiom in Spanish or Latin. So, she said to me, this time with a chuckle, "the old man is a typical member of the various villages, or settlements, that we have visited and is representative of how they speak."

'How they use idioms,' I followed.

"Precisely."

"They are a far cry from using our idioms, aren't they?"

"Definitely yes. And we theirs."

The sun now had come to an angle horizontal to my own, in other words straight away from my vision and at this moment I saw a crow flying very low as fast as his wings could carry him, heading for his nesting place for the night. Day time hunting for him was over. Ani spurred her horse once more and we trotted on. After a brevity we slowed the horses to a walk and then stopped to allow them a breather. Feeling that she worried, dusk was descending rapidly, I asked if her family might nurture concern that she had lost her way. "No. They know I'm not lost. I know every crack and crevice out here." We kept on our way; the horses walking now, unhurried, in a sense sort of resting, because like Ani they knew somehow that we were close to the end of our odyssey. In the distance we saw still another settlement, the oil lamps sparkling through the windows, small little things, but precious in my thoughts, and I imagined the family now sitting down to supper. Soon we were shrouded in darkness, the bright silvery Venus in the west already shining with her gleams through the Aspens and high in the east behind us the somber Arcturus showing off its flaming red fires. Overhead I kept finding and losing the stars of the Great Bear. When I lamented that I had again lost them Ani with playful excitement pointed in their direction, "See them Mrs. Bravino. See them."

When we reached the gates of the estate two figures with lanterns waited. One spoke. 'We worried my darling. We are muchly glad that you are now returned and safe.' Then he drew her to him, her grandfather, and said they all greatly loved her. I would spend the night and the next day someone transported me to Padua by carriage. I lay in my bed that night and reflected on the rigors and thrills of the journey never in my memory forgotten. 'It's the loveliest day I have ever known."'

Chapter 5

ON THE FOURTH day of my visit my friend came to me with word that he must accompany his mother and father to the City of Padua to meet with friends who wished to pay him honor for his service to his native country. He apologized for leaving me, albeit for a short while, a few hours at the most, his apology unnecessary I assured him and they soon said goodbye and got into their shiny new automobile and started to drive away.

"Goodbye again," my friend called out as he rolled down the window. "But not for long. Nageo will feed you and see after your comforts otherwise."

I ate well, Nageo often going to extremes to inquire if he should serve more of this or that delicacy, with me each time remarking with the epitome of politeness that he was more than gracious to ask and that already I had sufficiently dined, that no room existed in my internals for even a tiny morsel additionally.

It was then past eight o'clock and darkness had descended some time before. Nageo bowed and excused himself, saying in the same breath of speech that if there was nothing more that I desired he must go and attend to another of his duties with dispatch, this being to light the gas lamps throughout the environs of the home, as well as lighting the lamps posted on the arch beams which extended over the prodigious iron gate that blocked and admitted the coming and going of vehicles. Worrisome to me was that in order to light the lamps mounted atop the arch beams Nageo would of necessity climb a ladder of some length to accomplish his task, dangerous for a man of his age and gladly would I have offered to do the lighting for him but thought better of it on considering that any such act of kindness on my part stood as a possibility of injuring his pride. Therefore, tired and wary after going through a lengthy and busy day I went to my room and fell into bed without delay, where at once, a deep and peaceful sleep seized and overcame me, refusing to lighten its grasp until with a start I awakened and looked over at the clock mounted on the adjacent wall. I had slept for two hours, determined by my noticing the clock hand pointing to the hour of nine, whereas I had turned in at seven. I hoped and intended to go back to sleep. And I did take once more to my bed. But I did not go to sleep, I couldn't. Strangely, but perhaps not so strangely I began to dwell on that great home and its numerous particulars, especially its massive chambers endowed of the most illustrious and somewhat mysterious furnishings. If the truth is here told these thoughts had visited me continually since my first tour with my friend but less incisively. "Such huge rooms," I recalled, "and the tall exotic draperies, immense of height and magnificent from foot to summit shimmering from an unseen draft. Who would not have reacted with awe at the statues of armorial bearings fixed in an attitude of battle preparedness and at the darkened hue of the rooms throughout, adding mystery to the aging family portraits that ringed the towering walls? Ah yes. The floral garniture. What subtle hands that pieced these delicate pieces into a whole? Endless allurements. I am drawn irresistibility. I cannot allow this night to pass without again feasting my eyes on such wonders. Giovanni will treat me to another tour, I am sure. But why wait? I am here alone with nothing to do and the opportunity is in my hands." Despite these racings of mind, I tried once more for sleep, a futile effort. The rooms, one by one in their elaborate raiment streamed as a force into my conscious without let up. It was then that I realized what I was about to exact, a duplication of the tour that Giovanna arranged and guided on the evening of my arrival. I arose and dressed, pausing long enough to think of taking along a tablet sheet on which to record copious notes of compelling attractants. With delicate quietness I closed my bedroom door, starting softly my descent down the stairway. It led to the great hallway which in turn led to the first of the many rooms that I was to explore. It was here that I thought of Nageo. "Is he somewhere in the shadows watching me? Was he perhaps told to watch me?" I felt a tinge of guilt. "Am I violating the trust of the family? No, I am not violating their trust. On what grounds of reasoning am I doing that? If Giovanna were here, he'd tell me by all means to proceed." So, calmed by this, my self designed rationale, I made my way onward, thrusting aside whether or not Nageo somewhere stood spying.

The first of the rooms, I admit, I entered with at least mild hesitation, but soon shed any such apprehension, and after penetrating further began to discover that all was not the same, not altogether what I expected, or perhaps on my previous excursion I failed to detect the more miniscule images that now piercingly caught my eye. The vaulting loomed ever higher than before, reaching for the stars I detected myself muttering. I continued from room to room, for a while counting the number visited, feasting on the rarity of the amazing visual drama that unfolded with each step—the walls, the vaulting, the displays of the finest collections of art. The floors posed not less than a fascinating study, consisting of a quality of which I could not readily fathom, yet saw they were of inlaid stone, and shone with a glitter, the result of the painstaking ingenuity of some artisan from the City of Padua. The windows were closed, which yielded an effect that I could only call haze, that which you see blanketing a distant mountain after a drenching rain in spring time or that of a lighter shade accumulated in a lush green meadow at near dusk. I supposed that it had formed from the gas lamps, then supposed I didn't know.

Very soon I learned that this phenomenal family was more than a family that sprang from a militia of warriors and from there evolving into the management of infinitesimal acres of agriculture—a vast estate gained by their participation in warfare—but were scholars, historians, erudite people of letters, given to saving facts and stories pursuant to the family over time. I say as much because momentarily I spotted a parchment of stone with inscriptions of the Etruscan peoples, by that moment in history largely extinct as a recognized sovereignty. Someone of the family, or a hired scribe, in an age past had meticulously written of the Etruscans and their contributions to mankind. I judged, but perhaps erroneously, perhaps not, that the Roscilli family had the blood of the Etruscans flowing in their veins and that answered why the notations on the parchment. I read that among their many achievements, the Etruscans were skilled bronze workers and made bronze pots, tools, weapons, and items of household use, and moreover, that they were as well, skilled in architecture and that during the height of their power conquered Rome. Of especial attraction was the scribe's insertions that Etruscan paintings were most colorful and vibrant and depicted huge gatherings where people often and joyfully indulged in parties and banquets and risqué behavior. It was my bent of mind to read more but the want of brighter lighting cut my inclination short. "I must move along," I self insisted, "so much to see and feel. I shall never satisfactorily cover it all." But I would effort myself to try.

I have not so far taken up what I termed the influence of the East, the flavor of the furnishings in not all rooms but in a substantial number. I saw it in practically every direction I chose to glance. Some good many ottomans and golden candelabra of Eastern figure were situated in various stations about, and the heavy elaborate material used as carpet flooring where there existed no inlaid stone was clearly of that vintage in style and character. The paintings appearing in most every room poignantly evinced traces of immemorial culture, demonstrating the creative genius of those people that rivaled Italian artistry of the Medieval period whom I with good reason held as superior to any in the vocation of brush and canvas. It seemed that I did not take one step without seeing some form of the arabesque, for instance, in the paintings on the towering walls, and on the furnishings, the metalwork, the pottery and on flower vases and table cloths and drop pads. All this I had seen before, I feel prone to emphasize, but without the astuteness that now ran through me.

As they had over the past few days my thoughts now had restarted to settle obsessively on the unopened door, the one that I had glanced on my first passage with Giovanni. Something had kept drawing me to it. This night I had gone by it three times, three times exactly, no chance of my memory succumbing to error and from there my probing nature had grown into suspenseful proportions. "What lies behind that colossus?" It was indisputably a colossus, monstrous in terms of height and width and thickness and I kept repeating, "What lies behind that colossus?" I had to find out, unable to longer bear the suspense. It was then that I pushed all other interests aside, the viewing of the remainder of rooms, and foggily retraced my steps to where it was hinged, seemingly daring me to open it and come in. I reached timidly outward, barely touching the shiny iron latch, as if testing to see what might happen, but there was no movement, not the slightest budge, there arising in my deliberation that indeed something of much guarded secrecy was lodged on the other side. To say that I at this point trembled from nervousness is an understatement of my internal feelings. My heart pounded. But nonetheless I could not resist the temptation to proceed, reaching out my hand therefore to the iron latch again and pressing with only moderate force, spontaneously gasping in surprise, "Ah," as the door slightly opened. I opened it wider, enough that I poked my head through and scanned the interior, seeing only a foggy mist, perhaps a substance of steely gray, I should say, the result of the gas lamps I speculated, but thicker than the mist that appeared in the various chambers that I had most recently abandoned. Sheepishly, I moved to the inside, hearing the iron latch click behind me, for a moment losing my breath. With quickened pace I hastened back to it, fearful I had gotten locked in. I hadn't. It opened with one slight touch. On the outset I could hardly make things out but saw enough to realize that I had ventured into a wealth of resplendent treasures, no matter in whatever direction I looked. The room was spacious, greatly spacious, containing a volume several times in excess of all other rooms through which I had traversed, adorned with an eloquence suggesting that someone, a person of inordinate patience and skill, stayed busy polishing and shining and giving attention to the minutest of details. As I moved further inward, the gas lamps seemed to emit a brighter glow, with the mist softening as well, thereby helping my eyes to better grasp the beauty of the never ending flow of man made achievements, some dating back to historic antiquity. There was an array of vases and urns, huge in diameter, and tall as well, that lined the walls on either side, reddish and pinkish, the dominant colors, again the Eastern influence forging onto the scene. Later, Giovanni explained that they were crafted of terracotta and clay, but currently I could not tell which, the reason partly due to their emplacement on a platform elevated as much as a tall man's height and more. As I drifted further and further, my steps falling lightly and cautiously on the rich carpeting beneath me, I became to a degree lost, my bearings somewhat distorted. In all the while I had expected to catch in my vision the great window that I noticed from the outside upon my arrival with Giovanni. I had looked for it at least an hour since my entry, keenly searching the lofting, sure that it was somewhere nearby. It was hidden in the obscurity of the mist. "You have carelessly missed it," I badgered myself. But mercifully the Good Lord stepped in and helped me, and if he did not act directly, he must have given me a cue at that split second to angle my face upward and as I did so there it was in the high extremes, grand and magnificent in every way that I expected. It was essentially a decorant, with imitation trellises of variegated colors fringing all four sides, thus meshing with the lighting. I now saw with sharpened clarity the images about me. At or about this intermission I also commenced to realize a transition in the atmosphere, the mist thinning appreciably for one thing, and the other, the fragrance of a woman settling into my sense of smell, though faintly, the fragrance in other words which she might use for gracing her body. Confused, I let out, "But how can I say this is so? There's no woman here. From whence does this intoxicating sweetness come that invades my nostrils?" Confused! I was indeed, but managed with little delay to strongly suppose that if the olfactory receptors of my brain hadn't stopped functioning the fragrance resided in that area of lighting just ahead. I had moved from my position by not many steps when at once my vision intercepted that which I recognized as an annex of sort, a large opening that broke to the right. Without pause I promptly entered. The whole of the setting was lavishly ornated, I instantly saw, the décor entirely feminine for some strange reason, painstakingly contrived that way I took it, the walls covered with embroidered hangings, the lighting somehow changed to a radiant pendant gray, imitation flowers and ferns abounding everywhere—heavily perfumed—the draperies proudly flaunting their magnificence, and even the gas lights appeared softer than I had at any time seen. "What is all this," I cried out in bewildered amazement. In the next evolving moments, I was to learn.

With few steps more I stopped dead in my tracks, aghast at the image before me, a life size portrait, bust and face, of a young woman of age twenty or less, whose beauty I must say was not a phenomenon easy to describe, but which was enhanced further by the string of gas lamps streaming upon her face. Someone had chosen to mount this splendid work on to a stage or platform of abbreviated height—some little higher than myself—, so that the lighting and the ambience of mist intertwined to give her whole visage an aspect of angelicness. "Whoever has lent his artistry to create these devisements is surely the best of those throughout the land," I instantly proclaimed. I could not remove my eyes from her great beauty, and could not have even if I wished to. "Have I fallen victim to bewitchment," I inquired of myself but said, "no, I will not accept that I have but will admit that in an instance I was obsessed." I surmised in the same breath that there was only a fine line of difference between the two terms. The emergence of this sudden drama was almost too much, engendering an overflow of curiosities: "Why have I come upon this wondrous creature, this young woman of mesmerizing beauty, Dear Lord, and why in the name of sensible logic is she here and has the family hidden her from public view for some strange purpose? And who is she, or was she?" These things I continued to ask, at the same time astutely aware that so far Giovanni had not once mentioned anything of the slightest of this mystic person.

I must tell you that even though I fought against it my obsession grew stronger and stronger. As I studied the face in that portrait and the adorable subtle gentle smile, it got so that she more and more grew life like, seeming, as peculiar as it was, on the edge of wanting to speak my name and start into conversation and in the make up of my own psyche I each time found myself on the verge of speaking her name too. "Ah, fantasy, am I going mad?" I found the answer in my own strength. "No. calm yourself. You have not lost your good senses, you are not drifting toward the edge, nor are you seeing an apparition. You are simply obsessed. And what man wouldn't have that happen to him with a beauty like this one in his midst?" It was getting late and I knew that but I did not leave, I could not leave, gripped by that kind and gentle and lovely and imponderable beautiful face with the barely visible smile. Her beauty beheld me, I must attest, but there was something more compelling in it that wouldn't quite let me understand, and then, I remembered Madame Bravino's narrative that she prepared upon the return of Ani and herself from their all day excursion over the vast lands of the family estate. "As she slept, she seemed so at rest as I looked down upon her, so much at peace with the world, her breast lifting and descending with silent ease, her face that of an angel and then it struck me. Don't they say that she is not only beautiful? She is spiritually beautiful. And that is the greatest beauty of all."

"Spiritually beautiful," I called out in complete agreement. "Yes. Exactly the perfect description."

Time passed. An hour. Perhaps more. I had begun to study that face more intently, seeing now the spiritual beauty with unequivocal clarity that Madame Bravino had so capably committed to print. I saw this beauty, but commenced to see something else, certain strains of familiarity I will say, a feeling that I had met her somewhere and at some time before which my intellectual senses protested that such an envisioning amounted to nothing less than a fantastical absurdity. But was it? I drifted back. "I have seen her before. I swear. But where? I know I have. Ah! Yes. I have it. Right under my nose. Ani's distant cousin, the one who went mad because of his passion for his relative, but before succumbing to madness, I take it, set down a most remarkable description of that young lady, such that I can only kneel to his brilliance and hereby repeat a portion or two of his lines which are duplicates in description of this marvelous creature here."

'There is that immaculate face, smooth and without flaw, and then her sweet mouth, indeed the triumph of all things Heavenly. Do I dare omit other features? I do not. The hue of her eyes is the most brilliant of black, her skin luminously white and lovely.'

It was soon or immediately after this that I regressed to the masterful wordings in full that Ani's distant cousin had created, going back then returning, going back then returning, remembering every line, every word—how many the times—, whereupon at some interval it swelled within me as if a slow boiling cloud that I was upon a discovery most startling, a shock, to speak of it more truthfully. "This is not real," I cried out. "No, it it is not, but it is. It's, it's, gracious Good Lord. This is indeed Ani, her and no other that peers so beautifully out at me. Heavens! My breath is taken away. Am I to believe the unbelievable? You are. This is Ani, her and no other."

Indeed, I bordered on shock. It was as if she had come back to life—she looked so amazingly real, so life like, and now I not only saw the beautiful face but knew its name as well—, and by the twist of mind I was not but a step away from contriving that I had known her at another time, and that now we had met again. Of course, that was the wildest sort of delusion, pure fantasizing, but that is what the mind often does. There however was a truth about her and myself that I could not label as fantasy, her name, I had discovered her name and when my eyes fell upon her my natural tendency was to call her Ani. And from thence forward that is who she was. And then I returned to the earlier curiosities, which at no time had left me. I shall in due course address them to Giovanni, I said, the crucial ones especially. I will say to or ask him after telling him of my discovery, "Giovanni, my dear friend, "of what duration of years or decades has Ani remained in that room, and why is she there to begin with? Is it perhaps the people harbor a fear deep in their internal recesses that some day a drought wrought with famine may rise up and invade the land as once was so, drying up the crops and rendering the rivers and lakes barren of water, that she is kept there alive in portrait, and that if she is, even in portrait, they are safe. Foolish reasoning, you may think, but I am inclined to suspect there is a thread of truth in my words." As I have earlier stated the hour was getting late, into the wee hours, and I felt the compulsion to say good night to Ani, and I did bid her goodnight, once, twice, thrice, who knows the number, each time going as far as the heavy door with the iron latch, but then turning around and going back. Such was the power of her lure, but there was a last time—because my energy was spent and I reeled from the lack of sleep. So, I made my way outward to the heavy door with the iron latch, opening it and passing through, then from there crept as lightly as a mouse up the stairways to my room, disrobing as quickly as my fingers could manage and plummeted into bed.

Chapter 6

I AROSE LATE, AT the hour of nine, the butler Nageo calling through my bedroom door that breakfast was soon to get underway and that the entire family was presenting themselves, this including Giovanni's brother and sister who had returned from London, England. Upon hearing Nageo's announcement I instantly made my way to the bedroom window and peered downward, remembering, or was fairly sure I did—my mind yet foggy from lack of sleep—that I left my bed and saw that a car had driven up in the late hours and parked in the driveway. But now, the car no longer appeared where it was formerly emplaced. A strange one rested under the pavilion which belonged to the children who had come home from their travels. Nageo had moved the car from the driveway soon after sunrise alongside the other vehicles.

I descended the steps to the main floor and from there crossed into the dining room where the family sat already waiting for me.

As I approached my place, the seat on Mr. Roscilli's right, he lifted himself smilingly and promptly introduced Giovanni's brother, a youth slightly older than Giovanni and I, slender and handsome, as was his brother. Mr. Roscilli alluded to him as Petard, a Russian name it sounded, and curiously I immediately began to ponder why a member of an Italian family was bestowed a name of the Russian culture. Next came the sister, Mr. Roscilli addressing her as Pier Angelica, a quite beautiful girl, her smile somewhat subdued but friendly. It was a charming smile in any event, and helped to enhance her beauty. I looked with cautious glances at her throughout breakfast, hers meeting mine a time or two, if not moreso, no, quite frequently, and when they did, knowing that I had caught her, timidly she altered her face downward pretending to study the food on her plate. It was with the keenest within me to discover the slightest of resemblance of Ani—the eyes, the contour of her nice neck, the whitish skin, the natural charm—which were apparent but only slightly and were far from equaling the face in the portrait that I had seen the night before. I wondered of the strength of genealogy. "Can genes carry forward over a span of so lengthy of time to replicate the likenesses of kindred?"

Rolande, Ani's father, shot vividly into my imagination, a member of the Roscilli family in the distant past, who as far as I knew never produced offspring through Louisa but he didn't have to for his seed to show up in Pier Angelica. And the same was sayable about Ani. She was a Roscilli too and while she might not have ever married, the fact of which I did not possess at that intermission, the seed that begat her flesh nevertheless still lurked in the family chain waiting to crop up in someone even if in decades or centuries later. Mr. Roscilli, a scholar in his own right, was about to deliver a history lesson, and it was obvious that it was done to benefit me and looking directly into my face, as if I were the only pupil at the table, he at once commenced.

"We are a family that reaches far back in time, at least into the Renaissance period. The early members were soldiers, fighting in the Great Italian Wars, wars that are referred to as the Great Wars of Italy—and sometimes as the Hapsburg–Valois Wars—a long series of wars fought between 1494 and 1559 in Italy during the Renaissance period to which I have alluded. Let us ask this, because it is crucial. Why did the Italian Wars start? I am of the opinion you have already guessed it or in fact know a great deal about it through your readings of history. Of course, the desire for power and dominance set them off, essentially a mighty struggle between the Spanish and French, resulting with the Spanish dominating Italy. In time the Spanish stranglehold lessened and the power shifted from Italy to Western Europe, the beginning of this shift occurring, you might say, when the Great Wars came to a climax in the year 1559. Wars are a terrible thing, my boy, a monster bent on devastation and human bloodshed, never in the end proving anything except that mankind, if not carefully policed, will commit the most awful follies. Aside from this, that is, the devastation and human bloodshed, the Great Wars brought forth another folly, one of the world's greatest calamities, the creation of a situation that led to the end of the cultural flourishing of the magnificent Renaissance. At this time Italy was governed by a number of City states, some of them the largest and richest cities in all Europe; Florence, Milan, Venice, Naples and Rome, and that is why the more powerful, the French and Spanish sought to invade and conquer them."

He paused but little, appearing to shift his concentration not away from the subject at hand but approaching it from a different stance. And I bent a mite forward in my chair so as not to miss a single word.

"Now I have given you a capsule summary of a time in Mother Italy when warfare erupted constantly over a lengthy span, and my heart is saddened that the Roscilli's were in the midst of it all, or so say the documentations stored in our archives. Some were ruthless and quite terrible. Pillaging, killing, annihilating. I cannot refute it. It is so. The record is in print. And their story did not end with the end of the Great Wars, for there were other wars that followed and the Roscilli's were involved in these too, for however long I cannot vouch, but can attest that after the lapsation of a goodly period warfare for them was laid aside. The soldier Roscilli's gave up their sword and became farmers. Quite a change, wouldn't you agree?"

I nodded animatedly in the affirmative.

"But they were more than mere farmers. They were agriculturists, scientist in a sense, supervising and directing the activities of crop and animal growth, not at all on mediocre farm plots but on far outreaching estates which they possessed, or had gained I choose to emphasize, through the deeds of their soldiering. This very estate where you are spending a few days, and where you lie your head to sleep at night was acquired as a gift to the early Roscilli soldiers for deeds accruing in battle and the provision of safety and protection to an overlord or King."

I gathered that his children had heard this synopsis before, but paid immovable attention and seemed to gain much from it. I knew by the manner in which they hovered around him that their love was unconditional for this man, speaking always in a tone of pastoral reverence when addressing him on any subject and especially when calling him father. I found it beyond my capacity even in the extremes of my logic that he carried the seed of a former warrior. Once, as he continued with an elaboration on his familial ancestors of long ago decades I squeezed in a point of interest. "Mr. Roscilli, was Rolande a soldier of violence and destruction? Likened to some of his predecessors?"

"Ha! You are thinking of our angel Ani, and that the person who fathered her into this world could not have possessed those tendencies. And I agree with your thoughts exactly."

At this he rose from his chair, the children rising with him, knowing that it was his custom to pray a prayer following the meal.

"Our Father who art in Heaven I pray to you for your forgiveness of my sins and for the forgiveness of the sins of my children, whom I love dearly. We know we are sinners, that we were born sinners, and are helpless to rid ourselves of this heavy burden, but knowing as well that with your help and guidance it can be lifted from us. And for this we fervently pray.

And Dear Lord, let me allude to our young friend who now sits with us, my son Giovanni's friend, telling him in your presence that we are a family of peace, and above all faith, and that we accept him with your great blessing as a new member into our spiritual family.

And Dear Lord I pray more broadly, to the peoples of the world everywhere, that wherever there is strife replace it with peace, and hate with love, and joy in place of heartache, and sweetness rather than bitterness, and accord instead of discord, and good health in exchange of suffering, and sharing over greed, and light but not darkness, and pardon in place of injury, and above all, faith not despair.

And Dear Father, I will close, as I always do, with the purest prayer of all, for it is your prayer:

'Our Father, who art in Heaven, hallowed be thy name, they kingdom come, thy will be done, on earth as it is in Heaven, give us this day our daily bread and forgive us our trespasses, as we forgive those who trespass against us, lead us not into temptation and deliver us from evil, for thou art the kingdom and the power and the glory forever. Amen.'"

Offering an apology for leaving Mr. Roscilli promptly departed, giving as his reason that he must see into a matter at one of the nearby settlements which was a part of the estate. He seemed to manage things under his governance without effort, with a style that was thoughtful and kind to the managers of the various segments of farm production he had employed, picking the right ones without error, apparently, for they obviously carried out their assignments with efficiency and dispatch. Giovanni said that his father possessed a rare aptitude to read people's character and ability before hiring them.

All through Mr. Roscilli's speech I continued to experience a touch of guilt, if not moreso, pursuant to my entry of the doorway that led to the discovery of Ani during the night past, suspecting that I had been found out. But that did not seem so as I studied the family faces. Finally, I summoned enough courage to make the revelation to Giovanni, this occurring as we strolled through the most wondrous garden situated slightly southeast of the family home, but perhaps more directly behind it I discerned after taking second stock of my bearings. I had not seen this beautiful setting before. Angelica was the cause of our being there. She had intercepted me earlier with the question as to whether or not anyone had toured me through and when I returned that so far the pleasure was not yet mine, she forthwith prodded Giovanni that by all means he must show it to me, to which he momentarily attended. As Giovanni and I walked along, I said to him, "Dear friend, I must make an admittance that I cannot bear to longer hold inside."

"Oh! Well then. Out with it. Do not longer leave me in suspense."

"It concerns my self guided tour of your home while you were away on visit to Padua."

"Yes," he replied in an air of nonchalance, as if it were of no consequence in the least.

"I went from room to room, each seeming more splendid than before when you yourself led me, and then began to dwell in my thoughts of the great door with the iron latch, fearful after reaching it of entering but at last I touched the latch and went in."

With this said, Giovanni broke into light laughter, followed by a smile of anticipation that came to his face.

"And what did you discover?"

"Among the array of things of splendor in that room I found the portrait, of human size, and I was instantly spellbound. Her beauty and angelic persona were of such that I beg to refrain from attempting to frame it at this moment into narrative."

"My dear friend you need not tell me more. You came face to face with Ani. I know your feelings. You said you were spellbound. So was I when I looked upon her even as a young boy and still am whenever I go in to see her, which is often. Even as late as yesterday for a visit of some few minutes."

"But you are not surprised that I went into the room of her presence without permission."

"Permission! You needed no permission. You are my guest. Why might you need permission? You are free to meander through our family home as you see fit, and I am immensely gladdened that you discovered Ani. I had intended to tour you through to see her, but just kept getting caught up with one thing after another. My apology for failing to carry out a well-intended courtesy."

"Thank you. I am greatly relieved."

"I am sorry that you were distressed," he said with obvious sincerity and went on. "And now with that behind us may I inquire of you this, because I am muchly curious: did you determine as you stood there with your eyes searching her every feature that somehow beyond the slightest of doubt she was one and the same Ani that you had been told of and read about?"

"At first? No. But then the awesomely well described narration of the beauty of Ani by her distant cousin began to seep into my brain and then I knew that the portrait was indeed Ani. It was impossible to think otherwise. And the description set down by Madame Bravino played a role too."

"You of course in your next step will ask me to enlighten you with respect to why she is there. And I shall do my best. That is your next question, is it not?"

"Quite. I do wonder of that."

"Then I shall happily oblige you. Legend has it that some years following the occasion of the terrible drought, on Ani's age twenty or thereabouts, a portrait was rendered of her by one of Italy's finest painters who possessed such skill that he captured her beauty down to the last tiny detail. But more than this. People who see her now and then, never miss a commentary of not only her beauty but of her spiritual beauty which he did not fail to accentuate. And her portrait from that time has been brought forward to this day. Granted, there was possibly an artist of renown who now and then refreshed the original with a touch up, or else did a new one."

"I entertain a question, Giovanni, that you are yet to come across but know that you are getting around to it."

"Ah yes. I feel that I will. But do go ahead and ask nevertheless."

"Was her portrait emplaced there, in that splendid room, as a protection against another catastrophe, I mean to say was that in the peoples psyche?"

"I cannot say how it was then. In this modern day I don't think we see her as a protector. We treat her more as a, let me think, yes, as a spiritual shrine. But we all remember the story of the famine, as legend has passed it on to us, and in some respects, deep down, I think we tend to believe she is somehow our guardian against it ever descending again."

Not to my knowing until after the fact, when Giovanni told me, Mr. Roscilli privately huddled with Petard and Angelica that afternoon to remark that it seemed the nicest sort of thing for the each of them to spend at least a short while entertaining the family guest before he and Giovanni left for their military base in France. Their commandant telephoned that morning that the extra leave he had granted was soon to end and that they were expected back within two days on the dot. Petard volunteered to lead me across one of the back stretches of the estate to hunt for pheasants, whereas Angelica said she'd offer to take me with her to Mass in Padua provided that Petard and I got back in time.

The next day with the golden sun rising over the crest of the hills to the east we saddled the horses and were on our way, the pointers tagging along, sometimes in front of us and at others in the rear, frisking about here and there, happy they were on another hunt. Within the vicinity of an hour, we dismounted in an area of a densely over grown thicket that opened into a meadow through which there flowed a creek. The day was yet early and the countryside alive with birdlife and animals alike, Petard calling out to me the names of specific birds who were issuing forth a non-synchronized cacophony, happy sounds I thought to myself, and it saddened me a little to know that there we were with guns loaded ready to take some of them down. But I kept that to myself. Petard pushed on, deeper into the underbrush, with me trying but not effectively keeping up. Suddenly he came to a standstill, saying cautions to the pointers whose noses were trained on a target not at all visible to me, but without question in Petard's mind they had discovered a covey of birds. Petard crept closer, cautioning the leader, "steady Andrew," the male pointer, and commenced to raise his gun, whereon at that precise instant there erupted an immense fluttering of wings, three pheasants rising with speed so fast that they were gone by the time I raised my gun to my shoulder. Making my situation worse they flew quite lowly off ground. But Petard, a skilled marksman and seasoned hunter fared much better, taking bead almost as soon as they were airborne, four shots ringing out from his gun, with three pheasants falling into the thicket. Andrew dashed over and retrieved the kill and delivered them to his master. Petard killed much more game, twenty by noon, I but one. I didn't care. I'd joined him just for the thrill of it, this together with the invitation. At lunch we munched on sandwiches and sipped tea that Nageo packed which Petard carried in his saddle bag. I could have eaten more but there was none. The physical exertion plus the fresh air had given me a ravenous appetite. After lunch we lay beside a brook and reflected on the morning's hunt but not altogether because in little short spurts, I took flight to that sojourn of Ani and Madame Bravino as they perhaps passed over this same terrain. "Hmmmm. Where was it that Ani lay under a bush and slept?"

The afternoon kills very nearly rivalled the morning results, the day's count exorbitantly productive, amounting to a sum of forty, practically all of it due to Petard's hunting skill and marksmanship. Vainly, he sought to improve my shooting ability, teaching me to anticipate the sudden flurry of prey from out of the brush and how to quickly take aim on the lead bird and the next and the next—but to no avail, for time after time I depicted no improvement, eventually quitting, with Petard enticing me to at least try to bag one more. But I was finished for good. "I guess not Petard. You are a rare shooter. I am excessively enjoying myself by just watching you." I could have said also that I was a veritable amateur in comparison.

The day ended, and so did the hunt, with a spectacular sunset in the west, and I thanked Petard for taking me, a gentleman of extraordinary generosity, likened to that of his father, feeling that I had substantially profited by being with him on an excursion which I suspected he improvised solely for the purpose of seeing to my entertainment. Dark was upon us when we arrived at the mansion.

Chapter 7

THAT EVENING DURING supper, Angelica, who sat next to me, relayed that Mr. Roscilli was detained and asked her to extend his apologies to me for not being there. Then she reported the most welcome unexpected news. It was transmitted by phone to her father that morning after Petard and I left for the pheasant hunt that the commandant of the military establishment in France had for no logical reason suddenly decided to lengthen our furlough by two additional days. Looking directly across the table at him I saw Giovanna breaking into the broadest happiest smile which was a facsimile of my own. Taking care not to leave others out, Angelica and I dined and carried on with multiple but enjoyable conversations for the longest, until near supper's completion, at which time she turned to me more directly and leaned over, "Will you mind accompanying me on a trip to one of the settlements tomorrow, where a new baby has gotten born. My mother has asked me to go and deliver clothing for the infant. I will take it most happily if your answer is yes."

"I've already said it in my mind. I'm delighted at the opportunity."

She smiled vibrantly and patted my arm. "We'll go in the car. The trip won't take long."

The next morning Nageo's voice sifted through the door to my bedroom, much earlier than I had anticipated and when I opened it I soon understood why.

"Sir," he said, "your trip is now somewhat altered, Angelica said tell you."

"And why is that? Something wrong?"

"Not exactly. I will explain. There was a downpour of rain last night, a deluge. I assume you didn't hear it."

"I did not. I must have been fast asleep."

"Yes. Well, let me go on. The road to the settlement is nothing but a quagmire, a soppy sponge. A car would do nothing more than bog down to its axles, so driving by automobile is out of the question and so too is going by carriage, which could negotiate the difficulty some better than an automobile, but not by a gainable measure. Mud would splatter all over the horses, as well as the exterior of the carriage and its occupants. So, you see."

"I do. But is the trip now cancelled?"

"No. Merely altered. Angelica has decided to make the journey by horseback. She sees fit to leave earlier than the predetermined hour, her decision based on the fact that the trip will now consume substantially more time. She wishes to leave quite soon. When you have groomed yourself, breakfast will await you."

As Angelica had decided we left early that morning, the clouds beforehand clearing away, the sun not yet high, riding horseback, two stately animals chosen for us by the equine manager, both animals calm and disciplined he had assured us. Angelica rode the red sorrel and I the strawberry roan. She sat so straight in her saddle, an air of dignity I thought, so lady like, despite the lengthy slicker in which she had enwrapped herself which stole from the riding attire that I knew she wore underneath. I had seen her in it just before we left, an acute reminder of how Madame Bravino described Ani on the outset of their journey together over perhaps this same routing. "She even looks more likened to Ani this morning," I remarked to myself. Now she was more open, more at ease by far than when I first met her, conversing fluidly, with outgoingness, alluding to any and all things, even to a hawk that suddenly flew lowly in front of us. But her mood swung sometimes to moments that were less gay and more pensive. She tugged at the package stored in her saddle bags which the equine manager had emplaced there, and looked over at me, noticing that I sat watching.

"Precious cargo. It's for the baby as you know and I must assuredly deliver it in good condition." Then she laughed a little.

We rode along. Nothing but flat land no matter which way I looked, a sea of sprawling earth unfolding before my eyes, as far as the distant horizon it seemed, free of undulations, great farmland, with but few trees anywhere in sight. The first tree line of significance stood ten miles away, so tall that they were sightable in spite of their distance. Petard and I had gone in that direction on our pheasant hunt, virtually in diametric opposition to the course leading to the settlement.

We had ridden still further, an hour more I judged, and the slosh had worsened. Mud in spurts had collected on the bellies of the horses, as well as onto our boots and onto our slickers nearly to the neckline. While letting the horses blow, I noticed a patch of small specks of it on her cheeks and took my handkerchief and carefully wiped them away. She sighed, and winced, and turned her hands outward, saying she visualized that she must look a sight.

"How far is the settlement from here?" I think I had asked this once before.

"Not far now. Soon we'll be there," at this, the morning sun subtly bringing a lustrous glow to her face, after my cleaning it, to which I heard myself utter, "Ah, isn't she a beauty?"

We got there. Small but livable shanties dotted the village, some of the women sitting on the front porch seeing after the children in the yard at play. Others on the inside attending to their day jobs. At once those on the outside recognized her, bursting out, "Angelica, Angelica," running fast to where we sat. A sizeable many had reached her mount even before she slid from her saddle. "Angelica, Angelica, we are so glad to see you," they said in excited voices, gathering her into their arms.

Then some other shrieked or nearly so, "Ghastly! The mud! The horses are clobbered with it. And you my precious. Let me have your coat. And please do come inside so that I can attend you." We were then walking among them to someone's house where they would strip away her slicker and wipe her face and riding attire with a dampened cotton cloth. In the frenzy I turned here and there in hopes of seeing the blackened kettles with flames ablaze around them, but saw none. This wasn't wash day. But in my imagination, I saw Ani there nonetheless, with ladle in hand stirring the boiling clothes, to which there rushed one of the work women with anguish in her voice, which meant, that this adorable girl, a Roscilli elite, must not stoop to the lowness of a serf. Amidst the bustle Angelica had forgotten to introduce me or else she was distracted by it all to such extent that she simply overlooked her obligation.

"Dear me. I almost forgot. I want all of you to meet my new friend who is visiting the family. He and my brother are on leave together from their military base in France. He at my request accompanied me on my trip here."

As common as they were they yet were chivalrous in their hearts and bobbed their heads and angled their faces in show of appreciation that a soldier of the military would take time from his high position to grace them with his presence.

Angelica indicated on our journey to the settlement that we best cut the visit short and virtually at once, but tactfully, relayed that a package was attached to her saddle bag and that it was for the new born baby that had just arrived.

"I have brought the baby some clothes," she said, in something of a joyous announcement, and turned and ran to her mount, who was by then cleaned and dried and retrieved the package and brought it to the midst of the women who waited anxiously to see what was in it. At that point the mother with the baby in her arms joined them, smiling broadly, and depicting the utmost of curiosity.

"May I hold the baby," said Angelica, reaching out to hold it in her arms?

Taking the baby from the mother, who gave it to her with a proud and happy smile, Angelica uttered the classical, "Ooooh. What a darling. What is the baby's name?"

"Vittoria."

The women hovering close resounded with the commendation of approval that it was a beautiful and perfect name, while gazing admiringly at the interest that Angelica had taken in the infant—and one was heard to let out that she would make a fine mother because already she showed that the right instincts were in place for mothering. Here, Angelica started to unwrap the package while the women wide eyed with wonder looked on, attempting to anticipate what was in seconds revealed. Item by item Angelica lifted the contents of the now opened package, beginning with a colorful pink and white blanket, a gown plentifully imbibed with ruffles, an assortment of booties, and a rattler, the color of which I cannot recall. The women, already peaking with excitement, let go with joyous outpour and continued to stay gathered around Angelica after the mother with baby in her arms had gone elsewhere, heaping thanks upon her for being so thoughtful and generous as to ride so far to deliver the adornments.

Angelica could not find it in her heart to decline an invitation to take lunch, giving in to the insistence by the women at large that staying and dining with them was a must, promptly ushering us to someone's house where already food was set out and waiting.

Angelica cast a sideward glance as we entered, which turned into a smile. I knew what it meant. I cannot recall with exactness the servings those good ladies set before us, proudly done, I might add, and overcome that the young Roscilli girl was among them, as well as her friend. The servings fell into two courses, firstly, a soup broth, they called it, made from herbs and potatoes, and secondly, there were pastry dumplings, something tantamount to a thin patty of dough rolled around pieces of boiled chicken. And then a cake, a sweet and spicy one I should not leave unsaid.

Angelica drank tea. I asked for wine.

Throughout the lunch I saw as I glanced here and there the women training their eyes in our direction, slyly giving us the once over, not knowing what to make of what we meant to each other but taking it that there was an affinity between us or else I wouldn't have come along. Figuring it was all right I supposed, one old lady sufficiently emboldened herself near the moment of our departure to speak a compliment.

"You're a mighty fine looking young couple. Yes you are. May God bless you."

As we started to mount our horses Angelica suddenly climbed back down, once more going among them chatting and exchanging words of blessing and well wishing, a distinction of high breeding, it ran through me, "exactly who she is, a quality of class."

Amidst cries of goodbyes and tears that flowed liberally down people's cheeks we rode away, the weather virtually the same, excepting I noticed the wind had picked up, even though slightly, and the ground somewhat drier, enough that the horses did not slosh about as much and were under less strain. They now stepped livelier. I didn't easily let go of the remembrance in which Angelica intermingled with the women folks, and how they loved her, "a replica of Ani's time," it came to me, "almost like it was with her a long while ago as set down by Madame Bravino on parchment."

We had talked with each other out pouringly on our way to the settlement, so I was struck with surprise that there was a tint of reserve which had begun to show in her demeanor. I couldn't have missed it. She hardly talked at all, glued to something it seemed. That wasn't like her. I wondered.

"What is it?" I asked. "Still letting it all run through you, is that right?"

"Sure. It left me down. I grieve for them. Their poorness, their lack of education, their precious little children, who will follow with an albatross tied around their necks just as their parents, never rising above the muck in which they find themselves. Very sad."

"Yeah. That's how life is sometimes."

Unlike me in the usual instance I could not think of a thing more to say, but thought to myself that Angelica was one fortunate young girl in that she was born into a family of great wealth, and definitely a family of goodness. We rode on for a while, her still rather silent, with me saying nothing either, just listening to the horse hooves thrusting into the mire, in the resemblance of a sucking sound. But it wasn't long until I commenced to explore a possible scheme for cheering her mood, realizing that if this failed to work then I was in for facing a long empty trip ahead. It struck me that launching into her social life might yield a solution, not into her love life because I figured she didn't have one, being a mere sixteen years of age. I got it right.

"Where all did you and Peter go on your recent trip? I haven't heard much about that?"

"Well," she started after pausing a moment, her demeanor brightening, "it was a great trip. London, we went to London, a phenomenal city, nothing like it, and then to Paris, also a phenomenal city, nothing like it either, but if I were to compare the two phenomenals, I'd pick Paris."

I chuckled, then, "Why Paris?"

"Among an avalanche of other things, they have operas and I went to see one. Oooh. Magnificent. My father said that we, Petard and I, must go see one while on our trip. He emphasized that the experience would add great quality to our education."

"I've never set foot in an opera."

"You haven't? Not ever?"

"Never."

"You have missed a very extraordinary thing."

"Tell me about it."

She started and I thought she'd never stop.

"To begin with, there is the Palais Garnier, then the Theatre du Chatelet, then the Theatre des Bouffes, the foremost ones I should point out, with the Palais Garnier standing ahead of the rest as far as I am concerned. There, they say, you will see some of the best performances in the world, and it's my notion you will like to learn that the Palais Garnier is a 1979 seat opera house built for the Paris Opera between 1861 and 1875 at the behest of Emperor Napoleon the third." She went on and on, full of rare bits and pieces of this famous opera house. "The heralded Amelito Galli Curci performed there. She took my breath away."

Not only did she remarkably describe the grand Palais Garnier, she made through her words my mouth water to peek inside, and to save my money and someday see it inside and out close up. I learned, through her intelligence and aptitude, of the features of that wondrous edifice which until then I did not know in the least existed.

When I had attained to an age much older, in my thirties, I indeed traveled to Paris on mission for my newspaper, my employer, and with a group of others sat in that very place to which she alluded. It was fabulous as she said. I have forgotten who sang that evening, shame on me, but have not forgotten the numerous beautiful images which my eyes beheld. I lifted those of paramount importance, at least to me, and stored them as a sanctum in the annals of my memory complex. There are a couple that I have especially clung to, this being the horseshoe shaped French auditorium in the tradition of the Italian theatre designed for the audience to see and not be seen, its metallic structure hidden by marble, stucco, velvet and gilding, supporting the weight of the 8 ton bronze and crystal chandelier with its 340 lights. And the Rotunde du Glacier at the end of the long gallery, fresh and bright, with a ceiling painted by Clarin—a famous painter—featuring dancing bacchantes and fauna.

Need I say more. It was all so daunting, everything on which my eyes feasted, grand, grand, grand.

But I have drifted. Let me get back to where we were.

"Paris is a unique city," she proclaimed with bubbly spirit as we rode along. "Unique in every imaginable respect. I love it. I am pleading with my father to let me attend the University of Paris in the coming semester."

"If he says yes, will you yet have to take the admittance examinations?"

"If he says yes. We'll see. But no admittance examinations. I did those at the University of Padua a year ago. The paperwork will transfer."

"But you are quite young. If my analysis isn't fraught with error, you were a mere fifteen when you enrolled there."

"You are correct."

"Well how—?" She cut me off.

"I finished preparatory when I was fourteen. The university accepted my transcript marks with no hitches."

She would have felt excessively embarrassed to have told me they, her marks, were at the pinnacle of the admissions applications but I knew without her telling me.

"I'll keep my fingers crossed that your father will give his approval of your enrollment at the University of Paris."

"Thank you."

"And if you get your way, what will you study?"

"Medicine. Perhaps specializing in surgery. Petard says that is what I should do. My father is unsure but underneath I think he's leaning in the same direction."

Figuring the time had approached when we should opt to something else, I suddenly felt the compulsion to mention Ani, for she had swept into my thoughts sporadically throughout the trip, alternating back and forth.

"There is something else that I wish to take up with you, if I may."

"Oh! What about."

"It concerns Ani."

"Ani! She is of concern to us all. I adore her. I wish I had lived at the peak of her life."

"I too have such wishes. What happened to her?"

"What do you mean?"

"Well, for one thing they had universities back then. Theology was in vogue in that era. She might have pursued theology. She was very spiritual."

"Might. Well, I mean she could have. But I don't know and I don't think anyone in the family knows. The documentations in our archives don't say either, hardly anything at all.

"Is that it? Is there anything else?"

"Yes. There's more. According to legendary theories she became a nun, purely speculative you understand."

"Of course."

"And aside from that, she could have served in the military working as a nurse on the battlefield. For the most part however I have to sign off that she just vanished from the youthful life that we know of her. That's what everybody says. She's a mystery in terms of what happened to her as she began to turn older."

"I see." I urged my horse to step a trifle faster, seeing that Angelica had edged ahead of me by a few strides, both of us beforehand dropping our treatise of Ani, at least for the time being. The sun had now dipped a notch or two. "Isn't it amazing," I mused to myself, "that you always are aware that it is moving but you can't see it happening not even by an nth of a thread's worth." The wind had evolved into a livelier disposition and the dirt road showed signs of significantly drying. Angelica looked pleased at that. We had stopped from time to time to allow the horses a badly needed rest, for we had come a long way from the settlement. Once, near the end of our trip, Angelica pulled her mount off the roadway to a pond where we watered the animals and let them rest again. We let the horses have free reign, going about as they pleased after they drank. She said they wouldn't run off. The lily pads and the bullrushes together with a growth of sedges had colonized in the water near the edge of the pond's banks, now unsightly, said Angelica, altogether different from their appearance in the summer past, when they were pleasant to see. Soon, she spoke that we must go on, calling her mount forth and springing into her saddle. I climbed into my saddle too and once more we were on our way. It was then that I asked how far was it to the mansion, because I could tell by certain landmarks that we had drawn close. She replied in a tone encouraging patience, that it wasn't far and that we had made good time.

Glancing back, inasmuch as her mount had gained a couple of steps on mine, she asked, "You are attending Mass with me this evening in Padua, aren't you? We'll have plenty of time to make it. We'll take the car."

"Of course."

When we reached the mansion, the gigantic gate of iron stood open, the equine manager there waiting, who had seen us coming, and Nageo was there too.

"My," he exclaimed, as if aghast as we dismounted. "You are splattered all over."

"Indeed," Angelica returned in a feign of amusement. "But you should have seen us this morning Nageo. We were truly a sight."

Supper was ready by the time I had gone to my room and bathed and refreshed, Mr. Roscilli there at the head of the table, with me sitting across from him. He asked if we had a successful and enjoyable trip.

"We did father," Angelica assured before I could answer. "The mud was difficult to tolerate but the folks at the settlement were very much gladdened to see us and the baby's clothes and such were received by the mother with open smiles."

"Good, good darling. Thank you for going, both of you. It was a gesture of kindness from the heart that we needed to manifest and it was done."

In contrast to the night before, he talked and chatted much less, as I recall, bringing up once again the Great Italian Wars, alluding briefly to the inimitable Nicolo Machiavelli, a political giant during this phase of Italian history, eventually banned by corpus delicti to exile.

"Let me see. Oh yes. It comes to me now," he said with a countenance of delight that he remembered. "Machiavelli authored many famous sayings, totally his own invention, but his most notable one to me at least was, 'Leaders must not rely on luck but should shape their own fortune through charisma, cunning, and force.' This, I must clarify, is not who I want my children to become. I happily see them in their future years as users of science and champions of humanity."

When the meal was finished and Mr. Roscilli had uttered prayer Angelica came to me that Giovanni had decided to go with us to Padua, at that instant glancing around for his whereabouts, looking intently at the doorway through which he might pass. Shortly he came bouncing toward us. Angelica then said a bit unpleasantly that we must move along, that we were getting a late start. As we were approaching the car, a new roadster that only Italians could build in that era, each of us aligned in lockstep, Giovanni hurried a step ahead, "I'll drive," but before he could slide behind the steering wheel Angelica brushed past him into the driver's seat herself.

"No! I will."

Giovanni, with loving affection for his young sister uncloaked a playful grin that danced across his face, and then momentarily glanced at me, at which time I had occupied the pedestrian seat beside Angelica. Giovanni skidded into one or the other of the back seats behind us.

We left, Angelica, it was clear, exhibiting an attitude of haste, this occurring I knew because she had earlier relayed to me, she didn't dare run the risk of her dear priest reminding her that if one is unpunctual, only by a yard or even by an inch, that person in his view is absolutely unpunctual. Looking over at me sitting beside her she depicted not an unhappy countenance exactly, nor not a happy one either, only distraught it struck me, inferring in silence that she blamed her brother for our not departing on time and all because he had devoted excessive time and effort in the grooming of himself, and Giovanni, tapping my shoulder and winking as I turned around said with a certain facial expression, "What can I do? Nothing, except keep my mouth closed and wait for these minor tribulations to pass. She is my sister; my baby sister and I love her with an immensity. She is Heaven on earth to me. So, there you have it. Soon, this will run its course and she will have forgiven me. She always does."

The car ran smoothly, magnificently smooth, for it was a magnificent vehicle, a new Fiat, designed and constructed by the world's finest engineers of vehicles of those genera, and the roadway helped a bit too, itself smooth, poured and pressed of selected grades of aggregate stone. We were making good time, now beating the clock as Angelica meant to do, although driving too fast, but yet was in all appearances a good driver, possibly a superior one, careful and cautious at negotiating curves, of which there were a few.

Suddenly it came swooping back, the day's past events on the road to the settlement for delivery of the baby's attire. Angelica was a master at controlling her mount. "A semblance of Ani," I reminded myself, "Ah yes, of Ani—I smiled the broadest of smiles—who shamed hers into crossing the shoals. Wasn't that a sight? It runs in the blood of the Roscilli women, does it not, strong of will, determined, persistent, courageous, brave, likened to the Roscilli soldiers of long ago."

Amazingly, Angelica and Giovanna had by this intermission fallen into a stream of chatting about various subjects, the petty turmoil now forgotten and forgiven. "Even the finest of families have their spats," I reasoned, "and this one is no different, taking their discomforts in stride as something simply ordinary and quickly brushing them aside, the way their wise father has taught them."

Soon we crossed into the outskirts of Padua, a pale of daylight still with us, with me twisting my neck to see everything at once, Angelica attempting where she deemed practical to help me out.

"There it is," she said, in something of a blurting while pointing excitedly with her left hand.

Chapter 8

I RECOGNIZED IT AT once, the Saint Anthony Basilica, alarmingly huge and encapturing as it stood silently in a quaint little parcel of town, a lovely setting. Lovely indeed. So eager were they to acquaint me with the many sights and allurements that Angelica and Giovanni frequently got in one another's way with explanations and descriptions. On the very outset I took notice of the bizzarrness of the architectural styles, how could I have failed to single them out, and asked Angelica to educate me on what I was seeing but only vaguely understood. She would later on in the tour take up the architectural styles, all five of them, that prevailed to the sight of visitors but for the moment, stressed in particular that this Holy Church was dedicated to Saint Anthony, a patron saint of the lost, for people who had lost something regardless of what it was —but that Catholics equally set apart the Tombe where

Saint Anthony lay at rest. As we strode deeper into that vast edifice my eyes bulged with wonder at that which lay before me, the chandeliers, often ornate, of great immensity, the murals of all shades and colors affixed to the walls by master artists of the Renaissance period, the vaultings reaching to enormous heights, the sculpturing's teaching the lessons of humanity by their various configurations, the paleness of lighting in the chambers and antechambers, the quietness— mysterious, fascinating, deafening.

"Mercy," I let out, "this strangely grips me."

"Strange!"

"Quite. I cannot fathom the things I see and sense. I am unsteady."

"You say strange. And unsteady. You should not feel either. This is a place of peace and worship. Your heart should overflow with brightness, not with apprehension and downcastness."

"I know. But so be it. I will get hold of myself and in the meanwhile tell me more and show me more."

"I will, I promise you I will, and since we will soon take Holy Mass together, I think that is a good beginner, so—."

She seemed as if pondering, then went on.

"There are two fundamental principles that apply upon which our behavior and attitude rest, the first being that church is sacred space, the Lord's house, where we come to worship God together, and second, Mass is a holy and sacred act during which graces and merits are applied to our souls. And with this said I deem it well and absolutely important that I add and emphasize that the manner in which we approach the altar for Holy Communion is founded in the truth that the Eucharist is really the body, blood, and divinity of our Lord Jesus Christ."

I stood relatively frozen at the grasping and knowledge that this young girl possessed of the tenets of Catholic spirituality. But on the other hand I supposed that I understood whatever she had expressed suitably well, for it was essentially the same doctronology uttered by my old minister Sunday after Sunday back home. So, in the main, I declared silently, if there were differences between mine and hers, our Communions, they were at best minimal and I proclaimed that the Lord was okay with mine, as well as hers, and that he minded not in the least my presence in his Holy Shrine. I did recall aloud that I had always heard it said, and sometimes saw in print, that Catholics maintained the policy of kindly asking non-Catholics to abstain from partaking of Communion as offered by the Catholic Church. She paused but little with her reply.

"Bah. Brush that aside. We are children of the same Lord and Giovanni and I will stand or kneel beside you this evening as we take Mass together."

We had a while to spend before Mass, thus there was an opportunity to explore Saint Anthony's further, exceedingly further, for there were yet a plethora of things on Angelica's itinerary, though we could not leave from where we were until Giovanni showed himself, who had strayed away into that vast labyrinth and its attendant quadrants in search of novelties that attracted his inquisitiveness. Not unexpectedly he within minutes flashed into view, smiling broadly and happily, walking toward us.

"There you are dear brother. You are as elusive as a shrew. Please join us. We need to help our honored guest realize to the maximum all that which he is capable of absorbing."

"Yes of course. What will you have me do?"

"Just tag along with us, and intervene where you deem it productive."

We kept at it. It is not within my reach to describe in detail the endless man-made creations, rich and lavishly deep, aligning the hallways, the stairwells, the plazas, the mezzanines—everywhere and anywhere—too many and too complex for me to have digested and retained. So, we kept on, and I did my best, calling a halt eventually to inquire again of the architectural types of the Basilica to which she had earlier alluded.

"Forgive me my dear friend. In truth I was soon to get around to that very thing. And now I will take it up, not delaying one second's worth. Yes, Saint Anthony is endowed of five different styles, as I think I earlier mentioned, Romanesque, Gothic, Byzantine, Renaissance and Baroque, all existing contemporaneously throughout this Holy Shrine, all somehow woven together, and yet that is not entirely so. They are distinct from one another if one knows what to look for, not too baffling, I wish to add, in that they were designed, constructed, shaped, and colored in different centuries of the past, perhaps overlapping a shade. But about that I beg to plead ignorance. Perhaps the archives will tell."

Time had become our adversary.

"You must come in another period to see us, when I can take up where now, or virtually now, I must halt the tour owing to Mass."

"Yes. Of course. Mass."

"But if you will, I can still in a wee time frame go over a number of things of rare interest. Highlights in other words, but quickly done. Agreed?"

"Completely."

With excitement in her voice as much as it was when we first entered the doors to the Basilica she began to introduce me to this or that, more than this or that, all wondrous whether seeable or explained. She had by that juncture led me to the outside where a broadside view of the sights was more attainable, not missing a single advantage, and it instantly occurred to me that the high management of the Basilica would do themselves well were they to hire her as a guide.

"The Basilica is adorned with two bell towers," she explained with a vigor of animation in her voice, "together with eight domes, the central one measuring sixty meters in height." And then she led me back to the interior.

"The chapel of Saint James," she said enthusiastically, reinforcing her phrasing with the movement of her hands, "is in the Gothic style as you see, the frescoes done by Alticheroda Zevio, and the true heart of the Basilica is over there, the Tombe of Saint Anthony. The chapel of the Blessed Luca stands adjacently where he is buried in the grave next to the Tombe of Saint Anthony, his mentor and friend. I must not by any particle omit the chapel of the Black Virgin, the original core of the Basilica, the ancient church of Saint Maria in which it is said Saint Anthony prayed."

She for a brevity went on and on showing and explaining. Then suddenly halted herself. "Time is up. We must absolutely go. Mass is on the verge of getting underway."

It was held in a space fettered with murals and icons, and drooling with a spiritual ambience, spacious enough for admitting a sizeable throng of worshipers. Somehow, Angelica and I, due to the constant scrouging of the people got separated, such that she was forced to find a seat a few pews from where I had found one. Giovanni had managed to seat himself near the back. The people, I must mention, were extra friendly, seeming to sense or recognize that among them there sat a person unaccustomed to taking Mass, one definitely not Catholic, doing their best to make me feel welcome and at home. Prior to the beginning of the commencement of Communion the priest who spoke a potpourri of languages, though today in Latin, read from scripture a sizeable many verses, then following after him there arose an elderly woman dressed in a white and blue dress that flowed downward to her ankles while strands of gray coursed down her back. She too read from scripture and in Latin. I knew not what the priest nor the elderly woman read since I did not speak the language, though I felt that I interpreted with a measure of accuracy the conveyance of messages because I listened intently to their intonations.

With the completion of the readings the priest moved to the front of the congregation and started the procedures of Mass, aided by an acolyte passing a chalice of wine together with a wafer to each worshiper coming to him. Among other ministerings, the priest, it appeared to me, uttered a blessing in Latin for the soul of the worshiper. As congregate members began to rise from their seats in my midst, I realized that I must decide whether or not to participate in the ceremony, now standing and in a state of not knowing what to do, confused in other words, not at all unnoticed by a kind lady rising beside me, whose precious face I shall never forget.

"I'm not sure that I'm welcome to do this," I exclaimed, virtually stuttering, starting to sit back down.

"Oh honey! Goodness! Sure you should. We are all God's children and this is his house." And taking my arm she led me to where the priest and the acolyte stood administering Communion and when the both of us had there finished, led me to the alter, where we knelt together. I paused before offering prayer, out of an instinct of curiosity glancing over at her. How fervently she prayed, I thought, her lips barely moving and eyes closed with face uplifted toward the icon Mary. Shortly, she lifted herself and quietly went away. Just before rising from my knees a soft little hand touched my shoulder, with me of mind that the kind lady had returned. She hadn't. It was Angelica.

"I'm sorry I got lost from you. The people were thick. I wished to kneel beside you. I see by the lady just left that you had someone who did that for me. I'm glad. I have not yet prayed, so please forgive me while I go and kneel at the altar."

Without additional remarks she removed her top coat, a cloak actually, and handed it to me for temporary keeping, leaving only for my eyes an astoundingly beautiful piece of work, or art I should say, a dress ware or gown of old Italian lace, doubtless once Ani's, old, quite old, and I speculated in an instant that it had resided dormantly and quietly over the eons in the family vaults until Angelica sprang into life, deciding to wear it herself when of age.

It ran through me so easily as my eyes fell upon Angelica kneeling in prayer at the Holy altar. "She is surely a facsimile of Ani, Ani incarnate," I fantasized, "come back from long ago, and even that adorable clothing of old Italian lace in which Angelica is robed is fittingly designed to embrace the form and bearing of her relative. It's Ani's. I know it is. It belonged to her, was patterned and stitched for her. And she wore it in worship just as Angelica wears it now."

"Strange, all of this. Strange that I am here in this very place where Ani once passed among these medieval relics, saw and marveled at the wondrous imagery upon which my eyes have feasted, and worshiped at the very altar where her blood kin Angelica now worships. But strange most of all, is it not, that Ani seems somehow spiritually in our presence, and that all three, Ani, Angelica, and I have joined together at this particular time and place in His Holy dwelling. But am I hallucinating, or suddenly seized by a fitful dream that this is happening, and that there is a purpose at work in His scheme that I cannot possibly fathom?"

And then Angelica touched my arm. "Welcome back. You were far away somewhere, very deep in thought it seemed. Were you on a trip?"

"Sort of."

I promised that I would tell her about it sometime.

Seeing us huddled together Giovanni wandered over with a remark that we had to go, that we must prepare for our departure next morning for France and the military base.

"Of course, dear brother. Do you mind driving home?"

So, we left Saint Anthony's Basilica with Giovanni driving. As we traveled some few blocks away I turned to have one last look at that magnificent edifice, and with an experience stored in my system sufficiently in vividity to last a lifetime.

Giovanni, as did Angelica on the way to Padua, showed a tad of daring at negotiating the curves, tempting his sister in a play of buffoonery to issue warning.

"Watch out dear brother. You might injure the car."

Chapter 9

THAT NIGHT, GIOVANNI and I double checked our packings before retiring for bed, with the realization Nageo would summon us early for breakfast, at seven o'clock, and that Petard had consented to drive us to Padua to catch the train. After going to bed I failed to fall easily off to sleep, the cause being that whether foolish or not it kept recurring as an echo that I must go to that great room where Ani sat poised and see her face to face one last time, thereby rising from where I lay, then stealing slyly down the stairway and through that ponderous door and by not many steps further there she was, just as when my eyes first fell upon her. Beautiful. She smiled that misty smile, but not a smile, not truly, only the faintness of one, and gentle and lovely and alluring. I did not tarry long. Shortly, I said what I believed was my last goodbye ever, though I know not why, perhaps intuition and that's all, and she seemed to say goodbye to me too. I could almost hear her say that she was sorry to see me go. Then I left.

True to my expectation Nageo indeed called us at seven on the dot and very soon we had dressed and joined the Roscilli family for breakfast, something of a farewell celebration in actuality. I sat at Mr. Roscilli's side. He wished me well in his prayer of dismissal, thanking the Lord for sending me to them though briefly and to keep me and his son Giovanni safe on our journey.

The car roared as Petard touched the ignition switch, with Giovanni and I beginning to climb into our seats, but had not gotten all the way in when Angelica rushed over and hugged me goodbye for the second time.

The early morning mist pervaded the Roscilli home and immediate surroundings as we left, the condition resulting from the River Bacchiglione flowing close by and the freshness of rainfall in recent days. Its ponderous structure appeared immense in size and as we distanced ourselves further a misty fog had enshrouded the angles and jutting's of the frontage as well as the garrets affixed to the roofline. As we topped a rise in the earth the home now appeared as a mere silhouette and then very quickly disappeared altogether. Sadness came to the pit of my stomach. How could I have been affected otherwise? So much had happened in that brief stay which had lasted but a few days and I had drawn immovably close to the family members.

Petard let us off near the pavilion where passengers were waiting for the train scheduled for somewhere in France, which shortly pulled into the station, hissing in spurts, the hissing stopping and then starting all over. The crowd gathered around had waited for a length that obviously displeased them but switched to a more pleasant attitude once the train arrived and began to take on passengers. Petard waived goodbye from his car and drove away. Giovanni urged that we climb aboard in that the train had begun to give off a rash of high coarse broken sounds of warning which meant that everyone should climb aboard whose intention it was to do so. Not long thereafter the discharge cylinder, the smokestack, belched something likened to a swirl of jettish vapors out of its innards and then with a series of clanging and jerking the train pulled slowly away. Soon, we passed through the industrial district, then from there through the residential district, a settlement of small plain houses built wholly without the quality of architectural finesse, and eventually into open country. Giovanni, sitting beside me, yawned and turned over, still sleepy and with little lapse of time fell into slumber. It wasn't long that I succumbed to sleep myself and slept for an our I judge, upon awakening seeing Giovanni still snoozing away. Iron wheels pressed hard upon the iron tracks that lay affixed to the earthen bedding beneath us, throwing up a noise that resembled whoom, whoom, whoom with spaces in between. The rumble of the train receded into the outlying valleys, this accompanied off and on by a woo woo, standard practice when approaching a railroad crossing. Time wore on. We had traveled a goodly piece into the heartland, the passengers by this stage ceasing their chattering in favor of low inaudible murmurs. They had tired. All was relatively quiet and as my eyes swept across the lovely countryside my thoughts flew backwards. "I remember exactly my feelings when Giovanni and I first passed through that monstrous iron gate together, and how his parents lovingly received us, and how before supper Giovanni treated me to a grand tour of the home's many annexes and chambers. And ah yes, the story he told to me of Ani, the miracle baby, and that she grew into a beauty which I saw for myself in the magnificent portrait. I cannot forget of course Madame Bravino who so aptly described the trip by horseback that she took with Ani across a stretch of the family estate. And then there was Angelica, Ani's descendant, with whom I went to deliver the baby's gifts. Among all these there was Saint Anthony's Bascilica, awesome at first sight, and equally awesome as Angelica led me through. I will continue, I know, to recall all these things from time to time, for a lifetime I will, and many others that instantly do not now come to me."

The train ploughed onward toward our destination, Giovanni yet asleep, but seemed as if awakening. When he had come to himself a bit, not fully, he looked out the window and yawned, studying the contour of the landscape for a while, most singularly a small river that flowed parallel to the railroad trestle, the name of it in French of course. I failed to copy the wording in English that he foggily translated. At last, he was suddenly inspired into a state of animation and we commenced to talk back and forth.

"I've not told you yet, your being asleep and all, how wonderful my stay at your home, Giovanni. I've thought about it for the last several miles."

"I'm very glad to hear that my friend. We'll have to do it again."

"Yes indeed, anytime," I replied with emphasis.

"And what mostly moved you about your visit?"

"Everything."

"Ha, ha, ha." I figured on such an answer. But a good one."

"To tell you the truth my friend, when you asked me, invited me, to come with you to your wonderful home I realized not in the tiniest what was in store for me. Astonished is not a strong enough word. I shall never forget it, even if I live two lifetimes. I do hope that sometime I may visit again."

"I'll count on that."

"But not soon. I mean to say that we're unlikely to receive the commandant's okay for another furlough until some considerable passage of time. A year maybe. Maybe two."

"Two years! Cross my heart! Momma Mia! Those are most unpositive words."

"I'd like to have said different ones. But I couldn't. As you know we're just beginning with the therapies. Thousands of soldiers were wounded and await medical recuperation with aid from guys just like you and me. That'll take months, a bunch of them. I think we got our furlough as a last respite to rest us up just before the heavy work begins."

"No chance of an early discharge?"

"Next to none. Maybe far longer than two years, much longer than either of us might anticipate. We're conscripts my friend, draftees, and they'll keep us tied down as long as they feel necessary."

"As you sometimes say. So be it. We'll do as we have to, won't we?"

Among a host of others, that was one of the serious conversations of our trip back to the military base, I guess the most serious, but there was another which I had internalized of much less seriousness. But of much importance to me nonetheless. It had gnawed on me from the moment our trip started and now, the force of it broke through. "I must address it without delay. Our trip is nearing an end."

"Tell me Giovanni. I believe I've heard everything that is wholly significant about our lovely Ani. And you have supplied a great deal of it, but one thing yet remains a puzzle."

"Then I am obliged to assist you. What is it?'

"A person such as she surely had suitors, someone desirous of a closeness of her presence, or of contemplating a scheme for winning her over in marriage. Did I miss the mention of these aspects somehow?"

He ignored my question and began to address my preceding remark.

"I shall diligently apply myself to fully addressing the whole of the matter of Ani Roscilli, yet I am limited. To begin with I have heard talk among the older set of the Roscillis that she appeared to have no amorous interest in the young men who sought her. No one at all. And there were many, I venture. You are informed that she had a distant relative who supposedly went mad over her but who can say anything in the current family to validate that was so. It has been said that the Prince of Austria attempted to call upon her but was unsuccessful, despite his making many such innuendos. She was a most religious person, which I opine you yourself conclude was the case, and from the tid bits that I can gather she devoted her life to the nunnery, something my father and several of his predecessor relatives attempted to establish as fact through inquiries to the Vatican. Nothing ever came of it as far as I know. As earlier supplied to you, Ani seems to have faded into history without anyone in families much earlier than my immediate own knowing where she was or what she was doing when the Lord took her. We have only the limited notations in the archives to go on, together with an endless flow of legendary tales about her, as well as that mysterious beautiful portrait which hangs in the expansive lower room of our home."

Thereby, allusions to Ani with Giovanni from thereon seldom rose to the surface, both of us taking the position that there was nothing more that we could gainfully discuss. Giovanni and I worked side by side for three long years helping our dear soldiers return to normalcy, or to as near normalcy as therapy and medicine could make possible. Working with us were scores of other medics, young men and women, who poured their heart and soul into the cause, one of these a young woman of lofty aptitude with whom I became more than commonly acquainted. She was my superior. Her name was Sonya. As I watched her each day, she fascinated me with her ability to perform the most exacting medical applications and make decisions that doctors sometimes flinched at making. It started that way, admiration on my part that is, I liked her immensely, which began to grow into something else, attraction and from there to adoration. But it all began I must honestly say when I first noticed her.

"I am not blind. Her features, her smile taking precedence over everything else, reminds me of someone I have seen. Of course, I am playing charade with myself. It is of course Ani."

Upon my discharge I decided on a journalist's job with the regional newspaper in Paris, my exact working location in the little town of Saint Amand, south of Bourges. She came with me as our courtship had deepened and we married, not in any respect because there was something about her that so reminded me of Ani but because I very much loved her and she me. We knew from the beginning that it was a good marriage, that we were good for one another. She became my soul mate, I often said, and in particular to Giovanni with whom for long years I have maintained a steadfast exchange of letters. Sonya bore me three children and in my aging years they are adorable and precious. I have told her of Ani, all of it, and the Roscilli home, which prompted a wish on her part to go with me there some day for a visit or to simply look around. It was an idea of which I approved and relished, yet years have passed and we have not gone.

Likened to a burning iron the images of those few days with those sweet people have stayed seared in my memory, and sometimes in dreams I am suddenly back among them, Mr. Roscilli, Petard, Giovanni, Angelica, seated around the breakfast table with Nageo attending, and soon I excused myself, on my way to that mysterious huge metal door and enter. She is still there, the miracle baby grown up, that immaculate face, smooth and without flaw and eyes the most brilliant of black. The smile is kind and gentle.

I have spoken to Sonya as of late that I think it is time we caught a train to Padua, there renting a car and driving the few miles to the Roscilli home, hoping it is still there and the family well.

"I'd love that," she replied.

www.ingramcontent.com/pod-product-compliance
Lightning Source LLC
Chambersburg PA
CBHW070618310726
48982CB00001B/117
9780998852881